Scribe Publications
THE BUTTERFLY MONTH

Born in Amsterdam in 1975, Ariëlla Kornmehl studied philosophy at the University of Amsterdam. On completion of her studies she spent two years living in Johannesburg, South Africa. *The Butterfly Month* is her second novel. Ariëlla Kornmehl lives in Amsterdam with her husband and two daughters.

To my girls,
Laila and Emma

the butterfly month

ARIËLLA KORNMEHL

translated by Faith Hunter

SCRIBE
Melbourne

Scribe Publications Pty Ltd
PO Box 523
Carlton North, Victoria, Australia 3054
Email: info@scribepub.com.au

First published in Dutch as *De vlindermaand* by Uitgeverij Cossee 2005
First published in English by Scribe 2007

This edition has been published with the financial support of
the Foundation for the Production and Translation of Dutch Literature
Typeset in 11.5/16 pt Adobe Caslon Pro by the publishers
Cover designed by Tamsyn Hutchinson
Printed and bound in Australia by Griffin Press

National Library of Australia
Cataloguing-in-Publication data

Kornmehl, Ariëlla, 1975- .
[De vlindermaand. English] The butterfly month.

ISBN 9781921215261 (pbk.).

1. Women physicians - Fiction. 2. Dutch - South Africa - Fiction.
3. Women domestics - Fiction. 4. Female friendship - Fiction.
5. Post-apartheid era - Fiction. 6. South Africa - Fiction. I. Title.

839.3137

www.scribepublications.com.au

Part I

Two bare soles pointed in my direction. She hadn't heard me come in. She knelt with her head and torso under the bed.

'Zanele?'

Zanele startled and smiled; her eyes gave nothing away.

'Bracelet you gave, I put under bed.'

I stared at her, surprised. That wasn't the idea at all—she was supposed to wear it.

'I save. When I can't wait any more, I wear.'

After she'd finished hiding the bracelet, we walked back to the kitchen together along the path connecting her room to the house. She pulled her apron over her head and knotted it behind her. Her supple body began moving through the kitchen. I always enjoyed watching her preparations during the half-hour of each day we spent talking.

She displayed the food methodically on the kitchen bench. She had bought snow peas; she wanted me to eat more vegetables. With the pieces of chicken fillet in her hand, she glanced up at me. 'Spice?'

I nodded. I sat like a kid on an empty part of the bench. My legs dangled and I leant on my hands while Zanele took a plate, a wine glass, cutlery, and a napkin from the cupboard.

Again, I asked her if she wanted to eat with me, but she preferred eating in her room.

Later in the evening there was a gentle knock on my study door. I always left it open, but she still knocked as if it was shut. On the dining table I had left a book that Zanele, now standing in the doorway, waved at me.

'What's in book?' she asked, just as she did with every book I read.

'Oh … letters. I haven't started it yet.'

'Letters? No fun.'

By now I knew exactly what Zanele liked. She liked me to recount the stories I read. I read for two. Three years ago, my offer to teach her to read had been rejected outright. Pointing her index finger, she had said, 'You read for me.'

Early in the morning, I stood waiting with my hands on the warming kettle. Zanele came into the kitchen and took off her beanie. All morning, every morning, she would carry it around in one of her pockets; she never knew when she might need it. We said good morning. I felt her looking at me. Wearing underpants and a sleeveless singlet, I grabbed a mug to shake some Nescafé into. Zanele came and stood behind me.

'Too thin, Joni.'

It was barely seven; far too early to start thinking about something like that.

'You awake?'

Yes, I was awake, but I couldn't find the strength to respond. I poured the boiling water over the coffee grains.

'Eat something,' she said.

I shook my head.

Zanele wanted me to eat breakfast. A couple of times a week she would make me something to try to tempt me. But I didn't have any appetite. It was only around seven in the evening, once I was home again, that I felt like eating at all. I ate one meal a day.

Zanele did the shopping in the nearest town. If I especially needed something, I'd mention it to her. Sometimes she didn't understand exactly what I meant, or couldn't remember the title of a book I wanted, and I would give her a note to take with her.

When I wasn't working, I read. Then I was alone. Or with Zanele. I was used to her. It was almost as if we belonged together. Which was nonsense, of course — no one belonged with me.

One day I would tell her what had brought me to this place.

I thought she should know.

She had knocked three times on the big wooden door, wearing a dark-blue beanie. I didn't realise then that people here always wear woollen hats, even when it's boiling hot. I still don't understand why people cover their heads.

I asked who she was and what she wanted. Her response was to ask me a question. Could she come inside? I had nothing to lose, so I said I could spare her five minutes. She walked into the living room as if she knew the way, and told me why she had come. Without looking at me, she explained—in a mixture of Afrikaans, broken English, and the odd word from a black language—that she had heard that a single woman was living alone in this big house. That single woman was me.

Zanele wasn't alone. She had children but no house, and was flat broke; *platsak*, she called it. At first I didn't see what she was getting at, but she made it clear she wanted to come and live here and look after me. I suddenly felt very old. In exchange, she wanted food for her children.

She stayed for an hour that first afternoon. The idea that someone would keep an eye on me if I was sick or afraid was appealing. I said she could bring her children the next time, to see how that worked out. Zanele beamed.

I asked where her son was. I hadn't seen him the previous week. Zanele reached high above her head and waved with her right hand. I understood that Mbufu had finally gone north again. Somewhere in the north, in a village beside a river, lived the man Zanele thought was Mbufu's father. This was only the third time he had gone there. When she had told me about the man somewhere in the north, she had also waved with her right hand high above her head and stressed he had nothing to do with her little Shanla.

Physically, the children resembled each other with their long arms and legs, and even in the way they set their feet down when walking. But Shanla wanted to learn; she was curious and making good progress. By contrast, Mbufu was lazy—the way so many people here are lazy. He lay about on the street a lot. He lay about waiting, without knowing what he was waiting for.

Shanla could already write a little, and her reading was improving. But I didn't spend more than an evening a week on it. I had my own work to do, bringing the day's files up to date. She was happy with every minute I could spare her. If I was working at home during the day, which happened once in a while, I would sometimes hear her practising with her one little book. She'd practise until midday, then usually go and play outside. She would seek out other girls from the neighbourhood, and together they could play for hours without getting bored. They seldom had toys.

They would invent their own games with animals and trees. They tried to capture anything that flew — except butterflies, which were too beautiful. Shanla ran after insects with a glass jar in one hand and the lid in the other. When she finally caught something she would set it free straight away. I didn't see the fun in it.

'Just like sport fishing?'

She didn't understand what I meant. She'd never seen a fish.

In the summer they chased rats. They would race through the muddy garden at record speed. I didn't want Shanla getting too close to the filthy beasts, and I told her often enough. But she didn't take any notice — she enjoyed the game too much. If it had rained at night, rats would come to drink next to the house, and she hoped to catch one of these. The first rat I saw doing this — drinking from a puddle right beside the kitchen wall — gave me an awful fright. I yelled in panic for Zanele, who casually ambled over to me.

'They're everywhere,' she said to reassure me. I felt increasingly anxious.

'Just like people.'

I looked at her, in wonder.

Zanele began to smile. 'Get hungry. Make babies. Kill.'

Shanla wanted to know if she could listen to a CD. As the glimmering disc slid in, she went and sat on the floor. For the umpteenth time I told her she should sit on the sofa, but she didn't listen. When she heard voices and music, she asked if there wasn't also a drum. I shook my head, and she pulled a face.

I went back to my work—I still had one patient-file to go through. Shanla thought drums were essential for making music. Zanele had one drum standing in her room. With that single drum they played hundreds of different songs. Even in the evening after dinner, while I sat inside by myself, I'd often hear them singing. Usually Zanele played the drum and Shanla sang along. They had a whole repertoire. Maybe Shanla also danced in accompaniment. I didn't know, and I felt unable to ask.

We had never sung at home. But then, when were mama and I ever alone together? Only on Monday afternoons—twice a month—when I had piano lessons. First we would drop the others off at home after school. I was allowed to sit in the front. I could look at mama from the side, and it was only then, on these afternoons, that I could see what she really looked like. How the long black curls fell around her face, and how full her lips were. There always seemed to be a sort of line around her lips—not from a pencil, but a slightly pinker line in the skin around her lips.

She usually put her sunglasses on when she was driving, even if the sun wasn't shining. She would turn on the radio. If there was music being played and she knew the song, she sang along. I never knew those songs. When the news was on she listened attentively and gave her own commentary over the top of the radio. She would shake her head or curl her lips. Sometimes she would even swear, softly, so I couldn't hear; obviously having just remembered that I was there. She would sit in the car with her sunglasses on — the sunglasses that suited the shape of her face. My face has a different colouring and is less striking, but has the same shape.

In all those years, only once was I allowed to cycle to my piano lesson. Had to cycle. Normally she would never hear of it. The road was too busy and too long. The one time I had to go by myself she had picked us up from school and, after everyone else had been dropped at home, she'd said that something important had come up. I had to get out as well. I didn't understand what was going on. It must have been very important if I was to be allowed to — *had to* — cycle all the way along the highway.

I didn't ask what it was. I just nodded attentively while she told me I should be careful and stick out my hand when I was going to turn off and, most importantly, I should watch out near the small bridge on the corner by the music school. Before I got out of the car I gave her a kiss on the cheek, and could smell she was wearing perfume. She looked so beautiful. She was wearing her short brown skirt and sheer brown stockings. She was probably also wearing her brown shoes with the high heels, but I couldn't see them as her feet were on the pedals. What was she going to do? Was it a secret? Did it have something to do with me? Was I going to get a present?

I hadn't even shut the door behind me before she drove off.

I was dragged from my thoughts by the wind rattling at the windows. It was getting darker. Zanele hurried into the living room to close them. She had already pulled on her shapeless sweater and her beanie. A rainstorm, I gathered—a fierce one. Storms here could be so violent that I was afraid, afraid of the force of the wind and the power it exerted over the land. I closed the garden door in my study. 'Lights,' Zanele called out to me. Sometimes I forgot that the light should be on so we could notice at once if we lost power. I turned the computer off. Within a couple of minutes so much rain had fallen I could see the water rising against the outside wall of the house. It didn't worry me as I knew it would evaporate the next day with the morning sun—the next day, when the slugs that had fallen from the heavens with the rain would be happily crawling around again.

After the lights went out, I fetched two candles for later. Zanele brought me a sweater. It was the one that I didn't like wearing. It scratched.

That evening she came up in her floral nightgown, holding a burning candle in her hand. She was singing to herself. I wanted to tell her that I dreaded a whole night without electricity, in the dark, alone. But I said nothing. On the palm of her left hand she was carrying a plate with two slices of brown bread and jam. I would have liked tea with it. I asked her to wait awhile so she could see that nothing happened to me when I took a bite of the bread. She had to laugh.

'Yes, I know. White body can eat brown bread.'

But not a black body. She'd learnt that as a child. The fact that I wasn't sick after eating brown bread proved nothing to her. We'd gone through the same thing with yellow corn. I'd told her the whole world ate yellow corn, and no one got sick from it.

But, makes them impotent, she said. Whites were impotent more often than blacks.

'There is no difference between our bodies. I've told you a hundred times, Zanele.'

'Kkkk.' She clicked her tongue and walked away with a gesture that made it clear I knew nothing about it.

The God of Africa was furious for weeks. I pulled the sheet over my head. He became enraged every summer. With each thunderclap he left me trembling. He was close. I tried to count between the flash and the sound, but I couldn't; it seemed like one moment. The sheets were clenched in my fingers and my eyes were clenched shut. Tomorrow it would be over. Tomorrow I would see for myself. Tomorrow, when the slugs showed themselves in force and I could smell the scent the rain had left behind. And tomorrow would be the day *after* my birthday. Luckily no one here knew that. I didn't like birthdays. But at home they'd have known. They must have thought of me at home — thought of me without saying anything. Mama would have reminded herself of the day we'd performed well together; the day we'd both shown our strength.

But today she had shown her weakness.

The sheet was folded at the foot of the bed. It was too warm for sheets. I looked upwards. I couldn't see the ceiling. I knew it was there, but I couldn't see it. I thought it was creepy that I could switch on a light and nothing would happen. I turned my head to the side. I couldn't see the window. I knew it was there, but I couldn't see it behind the curtains. I couldn't see any curtains. Behind that window shone a moon that was concealing itself. But I knew the moon was very close — that you could grab it if you just stretched out far enough.

The storm had raged for so many nights in a row that I couldn't see how big the moon had become in the meantime. I hoped it wasn't yet full. There was something sad about the full moon. A full moon meant a fresh chance. Young men from bordering countries would pull on their shoes, tie water-bottles around their waists, and start out on a nocturnal journey to bring them to a richer country on this continent. The bright moonlight helped them avoid the border posts so that, pleased with themselves, they could slap their strong hands together once they'd entered the republic. But it was after this that their journey became truly frightening, and not because of the illegal crossing. The sweating men were making their way into a region inhabited not only by elephants and hyenas, but primarily by lions. The morning after the night of a full moon, one routinely read in the papers that a border guard had once again come across empty water bottles, torn trouser legs, and shoes. And still they kept trying.

But I couldn't see the moon.

I couldn't even see the hand in front of my face.

If things had worked out differently I wouldn't be lying

here. I wouldn't have come to Africa. I wouldn't be working and living as I did now.

Zanele announced, early in the morning, that she was going to the village with Shanla — now, before it got too warm. Did I still need her in the house? I shook my head. I did remember that I'd gone through my paper supply and asked if she could pick up a new pack. Shanla heard, and asked if she could buy pencils at the bookshop. While I was getting the money out, I said it was also for the pencils, and Shanla smiled.

Mbufu was staying at home, Zanele said. He was tired after his trip back from the north. I hadn't heard him at all. He was probably just hanging around somewhere. He was sixteen, and still he couldn't amuse himself. He'd made an occupation of boredom.

I sat behind my computer to finish writing a report before the evening shift. I couldn't work. I was thinking about how best to explain it all to her, to make her understand. She always moved a step closer when something wasn't completely clear. Then my words became confused, and the simpler I tried to word it, the more difficult it seemed. Where should I start?

I could start at the beginning. Or with Wouter. Yes, I should start with Wouter. Then I could say I'd known real love. Or would she laugh at me?

It was too warm for such a long walk — to the village and back — but they wanted to go, no matter what. Once Zanele got an idea into her head, there was no changing her mind.

They arrived home in the heat of the day carrying full bags. They never sweated, but always looked as if they had just been sitting under the big tree on the corner. Shanla gave me the packet of paper, and Zanele asked if she could keep the small amount of change left over. I nodded, and knew it wouldn't be the right day to say anything.

Anyway, I wasn't feeling great, either. I hadn't slept well and had started work early, once I'd seen that we had electricity again. With the coming evening-shift in mind I thought it might be better if I rested outside under an umbrella on the terrace. I could go on with the report afterwards. While I was walking outside, Zanele mentioned she'd checked our letterbox in the village. I raised my eyebrows.

'No mail,' she said.

There was never any mail, but still she always looked.

I let myself sink into a deckchair on the terrace. The strong sunlight was annoying, even with my eyes shut. It still amazed me how angry he was at night, and how gentle during the day. Every summer the God of Africa revealed himself this way. I tried to count how many summers I'd been here, but I was too tired. In any case, it was a few years. Years without mail.

With a short, gentle movement, he pushed the hair from my face. His lips came closer and pressed a kiss precisely in the middle of my forehead. I shut my eyes. I wanted more. I felt surrender, an intense sense of surrender. The kiss could mean he was leaving or that he wanted to make love to me.

As my fringe fell back on my forehead, his hand slid between my legs. My body got what it was longing for, and I allowed myself to drift into my unrestrained world; the world where everything comes from my belly, where I am awake while my head sleeps. It is a luxury, my surrender—first to him and then to myself. And again the kiss, pressed as evidence on my forehead above my eyebrows.

Screams woke me. Actually, it sounded more like crying and screams mixed together. For a second I thought they might even be singing together. I leapt up and ran into the house, through the kitchen, and along the little path to Zanele's room. Her door was shut, and that meant I wasn't allowed in. I wondered what was going on inside.

It was Shanla who was in such a state. Motionless, I stood in front of the door. Zanele sounded angry, but I couldn't follow her Zulu. Irritated, I walked back inside and waited in my study until it was quiet again.

Some time later, Shanla walked mournfully into my room. I was horrified. A short layer of hair covered her scalp. I asked her what had happened. Tearfully, she told me her mother had done it—there had been too many knots in her hair. She ran her fingers over the back of her head. 'Now I'm a boy.'

I pushed my chair back and took her on my lap. My right hand felt the roughness of her hair. Her eyes filled again. I tried to soothe her—it took more than short hair to make you a boy.

But she said it didn't.

The wild weeks were over. Zanele tipped her head all the way back to look at the heavens. 'Now go outside!' she yelled exuberantly. She had been looking forward to it for weeks, and finally it was time. She was going for four days to visit a friend who was from the same township as her.

It felt like they were away for a month. Maybe it was

because she'd taken the children. I couldn't see why they had to go away for four days right now. Suddenly it was very quiet at home; everything slept. I didn't sit on the kitchen bench in the evenings, and I didn't laugh in the mornings. I buttered a piece of bread, and remembered how we'd laughed about the pet ambulances just before she'd left.

I'd explained to her they were quite common in the Netherlands. She didn't want to believe me and, really, it was ridiculous. Where she grew up there wasn't even a normal ambulance, no matter how sick someone was. She told me about the time when her mother was dying. None of the medicine men could help them. Zanele knew that in the city a doctor would come. He would be telephoned. But if you didn't have a telephone you couldn't call, and if you didn't have an address no one could find you.

They divided their township into four parts so they could at least talk about an east-side and a south-side. In those parts you could ask for a specific hut, and usually you'd get some help. Zanele said her mother had died of a heart attack. I asked her how she knew. She told me that her oldest brother had said her mother's heart was no longer beating, so she must have had a heart attack.

I nodded, and saw her mother before me. All I really knew about her was how she'd washed her seven children, one after the other, with a cloth and a bucket of tepid water. Tepid, because she'd let it stand the whole morning in the sun.

Zanele had once demonstrated for me how they'd all had to sit in a row on her mother's bed. 'Naked, of course,' she said. Her hands at hip height gestured a small mound; the children had to lay their clothes next to them on the bed so they could put them on again themselves. Her mother would call their names, one by one, and wash them. She had a separate cloth for drying; but if you were the last, or even the second last, it didn't really serve its purpose any more. The last one dried himself in the sun. Usually, Zanele's mother would let one of the boys be the last. The big wash happened once every few days, and Zanele showed with a sniff of her nose how nice everything smelled then.

The pet ambulance! We almost wet ourselves. I had to laugh most at her exuberant laugh, her disbelief, and her surprised eyes. It was never long after we'd been talking about something like this that Shanla would come walking into the house with a mischievous smile on her face. Her mother had obviously told her about our conversation, but she wanted to hear it again from me.

They sat chatting while they packed for their four-day holiday, the door half open to let in the breeze. Zanele was talking about men. Men in general. She was spelling out for Shanla how she should let men treat her when she was older. And especially how she shouldn't let them treat her. It's true that the men who visited Zanele now and then did seem honoured to be invited onto our property. Not because of our property, but because Zanele had asked them. If a man didn't behave she immediately threw him out. Shanla learnt she should never let herself be conned, and she should never work to provide a man with money, as Zanele put it. The only thing you should be doing with the money you earned was provide food for your children, and after the age of two their food would cost money. For your children you'd do anything, but not for men. It was Zanele's conviction that men saw a woman as a temporary parking-spot that they would eventually leave.

She spoke like this regularly to her daughter, as if the repetition would make sure it sank in. I listened closely to how she tried to make these ideas clear, and in the meantime I enjoyed watching the supple movements that emanated from her buttocks. When she walked up the stairs her buttocks set the pace that her body followed.

Just before she left, she stood with one of my photos in her hand in the doorway of my study.

'What's this?'

I saw my brothers playing in the snow. Beanies and mittens.

'That's snow, Zanele, but I don't want you looking at my photos, you know that ...'

She started, and muttered that she only wanted to know what the white stuff was.

I didn't want her looking at my photos.

I never looked at them myself.

'In five years, all whiteys live in Soweto.' I looked at her, surprised.

'And you know what's handy?'

I shook my head. Zanele drew back her eyelids and began slowly to smile.

'Their stuff is already there!'

I had to laugh. She'd spent a few days with other people, and they'd told her this joke. If it was a joke.

'Good one?' she asked in confirmation.

It was better than good. When I asked her if she had any

other new ones, she said she was saving the rest. It didn't matter to me when she told me, as long as she stayed at home.

'Ah, now I see, doctor has cut hair!'

I felt self-conscious. 'It needed it, right?'

She asked me to turn around. She wanted to see how long it was from the back. 'Oho, not good!'

I didn't know a hairdresser in the area, so I'd done it myself.

'You shouldn't call me doctor.'

I went and sat on the kitchen bench, letting my feet rest against the rubbish bin, and leant backwards. Hadn't I wanted to become a doctor, asked Zanele, who had started cooking.

'Not really, no.'

I told her about my brothers, who were both doctors. The oldest loved to paint, but life as an artist wasn't an option for him. 'My father was a doctor. My mother, a nurse. She stopped working because of us. The greatest achievement, we were taught, was to *be someone* in a hospital ...'

Zanele set a glass of water next to me on the kitchen bench. It was a habit I didn't resist any more—she liked giving me something to drink. She turned her back towards me to prepare the chicken.

'*Be someone* in a hospital,' I heard myself say again. I remembered my father at work. As a six-year-old I was allowed to go with him to his department, his office, for the first time. I walked alongside him through the corridors, proud to be his child. My father let me put on his doctor's jacket. I almost didn't dare to, but Andre and Alex had told me all about it, and that had made me curious. I held the cotton as if it was velvet—and when I'd finally pulled the jacket on and buttoned it up, I was too afraid to move. It was papa's work jacket, after all. He told me that Andre had once come to his office and just gone on drawing. It annoyed him that Andre always took his pencils with him wherever he went. Even in the hospital he looked for a quiet place, and set to work with his coloured pencils.

'Andre, my oldest brother, is a cardiologist.'

'Uh?'

'A heart doctor. A doctor who specialises in the heart.'

I took a sip of water.

'He only knows about heart?'

'No, but that's what he knows the most about'.

She nodded and went to get the white rice. The water was already boiling. Getting the rice in the pan was difficult, as we could only get five-kilo packs. She always succeeded in throwing exactly the right amount into the boiling water from the heavy bag.

'And other brother? What sort doctor?'

'He's a GP. A normal doctor, a bit like I am. People come and see him unless they are too sick, then he visits them in their home to make them better.'

'Ah, *inyanga*!' she exclaimed.

'*Inyanga*? Isn't that the moon?'

'*Yebo*. Moon. But also doctor.'

'Oh, you mean a doctor connected to the moon? A medicine man?'

Zanele nodded, pleased I understood her. 'We also say *sangoma*.'

'What's that, then?'

'Witch-doctor.'

Zanele spoke Zulu with her children and sometimes with me. She told me what the average witch-doctor could do, how every village had one, and that it was usually a very old person. She bent her back to show how they usually walked, and put on a croaking voice. I loved it when she used different voices to tell me something. At these moments, together in the kitchen, I was no longer interested in a different life that I could have lived.

I emptied the glass, jumped down from the bench, and walked into the living room. I sat with my dinner at the silent table. Zanele took the same food for the three of them to her room. We were eating chicken with rice and beans.

I walked back into the kitchen with my dirty plate. I didn't turn the light on; I only had to put the plate on the counter. The counter was easy to find even in the dark. It ran the full breadth of our rectangular kitchen, under the windows that overlooked the outdoor paths. I shut the kitchen door.

The *inyanga*. I wouldn't have thought of it. I would have liked to talk to Zanele for longer, but the children had to eat.

I happened to see the admissions date written on the top right of a patient's file, and realised it was exactly three years ago that I'd come here to work.

To Zanele's annoyance, I still called my workplace 'the first-aid station.'

'Emergency,' she would correct me, muttering.

No matter what time of the day my shift was, it was busy. More misery, more people waiting—sick, raped, dehydrated. Lots of accidents. There were always people who'd been in accidents. Sometimes they brought them in already dead, without anyone having noticed. I was soon through with the so-called DOAs. Then there were gunshot wounds and still more gunshot wounds. We had a specialist for those.

I made sure everything was well documented. It often wasn't possible to do this at work, so I would do it at home. All the half-filled patient files caused delays and inefficiencies. But the problems were also caused by the patients. No surnames, no addresses, no details. 'Nil identity', Albert would write on those files. I usually tried to write a description of the patient I saw in front of me, but often ended up doing the same.

Nil identity.

Exactly three years of service meant my contract still had two years to run. After that, I had to go. I didn't want to go. Not back.

Maybe I could manage to work longer at the hospital? There was enough work; that wouldn't be the problem. I did little else but work. Not working to live, but living to work. Wouter had hated that. Life should be more. He wanted to see me laughing, hold me, and dream of endless togetherness.

We'll last, sweetheart, he'd once said as he pressed a short kiss on my forehead before closing the door behind him. Then I smiled. Scared, because I wanted it so badly.

Shanla had heard from her mother that I had only become a doctor because my family expected it. I asked her if she already knew what she wanted to be when she grew up. She didn't have to think about it for long.

'Maid.'

'Maid? Wait a minute. That's only because your mother is one.'

'No. Not true. I want to be maid!'

'You're not learning reading and writing for nothing. You can do better than being a maid. You know that, don't you?'

'If I'm maid, I always have house and food.'

So that's how she got the idea. I had to try to talk her out of it.

'If you do different work, you'll earn enough money to buy more than a house and food.' I tried to keep her attention; it was important she understood.

She looked at me, surprised. 'But being maid isn't difficult, and I could do it.'

'But that's just it! You could do a lot more!'

So she had thought about her future. I'd never really done that myself.

Shanla asked me what I had really wanted to be. It was pointless asking myself now. I said nothing.

Zanele came into the living room. She'd heard our conversation from the kitchen. She asked me why I didn't answer Shanla.

'When we're older, Zanele. When we're older.'

'But I'm already old,' said Zanele.

I didn't feel like elaborating. 'I'm still not old enough.'

Bare feet on the stone floor in the passageway. They were coming towards me. Suddenly, they stopped in the study doorway.

'Joni?'

I turned my chair towards her and asked what was up.

She probably thought she was interrupting me because I was sitting behind my computer with a lot of words on the screen—words from a patient's report. But I hadn't added a single word.

I looked into her black eyes for as long as it took for her to glance at me. I'd taken pains with this over the years; at first, Zanele had looked at the ground when she spoke to me. I hadn't realised when she knocked that first afternoon that it would stay like that unless I tried to change it. I'd thought it was because she was shy; now I knew better.

'I'm going to bed.'

I looked at my watch and saw it was almost ten o'clock. 'Oh God, yes, I must get going. I have a night shift.'

'Yes, I thought so. I'm going to bed now.'

Even though Zanele couldn't tell the time, she always knew what the time was. She worked it out from the sun and the length of time it took her to do certain chores. She told me her friends did the same, and when they all sat together under the big tree on the corner in the afternoon it was always for exactly one hour, although not one of them could tell the time.

'Good night, Zanele …'

'Joni?'

'Yes?'

'Not too tired to go to work?'

'Ach …'

'I'll make you coffee when you get back, okay?'

'Do you know what my father always said after his night shift?'

'Eh?'

'Your breakfast is my dinner.'

With a polite smile, she remained standing in the doorway for a moment. It wasn't much of a joke, but it was true; he often came home just as we were leaving for school. The black rings under his eyes went with his face, and I could see that best on these mornings. The first thing my mother would say to him was that she'd had to sleep alone. I couldn't see what was so bad about that; I slept alone, too. Andre and Alex shared a room, though even Miri slept alone. But Mama had to say it every time. Usually, my father pretended he hadn't heard; he would grab a slice of bread, and spread butter on it. That's when he'd say that our breakfast was his dinner. Sometimes he did respond in a tone that suggested it was the hospital's fault. 'What in God's name can I do about it?' She never answered this question. Because she so often didn't answer his questions, I thought there were questions that you never had to answer.

Zanele was still standing in the doorway.

'Joni? You thinking about the man?'

'No, Zanele. Will you drop it?'

She was dying to know what had happened with the flirt from the hospital. She didn't want me to be alone forever. She was pushing it.

'Oohoo, Joni's annoyed!'

'No I'm not, but I've already told you it won't come to anything. Mind you, it was worth the trouble, if you must know—fun, even!'

Her hand flew over her mouth.

I stood and walked towards her. 'Only once,' I held my index finger up, right in front of her face. 'Only once have I

23

wanted to live with a man.'

'Who then?'

'It's over,' I said decisively, to make it clear I'd finished with it.

She wasn't convinced. 'If someone is in,' she tapped her breast, 'he doesn't get out easily …'

I tried to suppress a smile.

To get her off my back I told her as indifferently as possible about a man I'd come to know during my studies and had lived with before I left for Africa. About Wouter. Although I didn't want her to think it was because of him that I had left.

When I told her he'd already had a family, I could see I was going too fast for her. It usually became clear pretty quickly when she wasn't following me, if she'd lost the thread—I could see it in her eyes. Once, in the beginning, I had asked her to let me know if I spoke too fast, or if she no longer understood me. She'd nodded, and indicated that she always understood me perfectly. Zanele was a proud woman.

She asked me how old he was.

'Not old at all; there was only a couple of years' difference between us.'

'But he had family, you said?'

'Yes, he was, as they say, "caught early".'

'How many children then?'

'One, a son. He still lived with his family when we met each other. He left after a while.'

'Oohoo! For you?'

I turned away, and thought about Wouter's son and how old he would be now. I packed the files from my desk. Zanele didn't budge, which meant I ended up standing with my back to her. I turned again, just to be polite. Her eyes stared at me questioningly.

'I really have to leave now, Zanele.'

With a long face, she walked into the passage.

'Goodnight,' I called.

Good God, that I'd just come out and said it was fun with Mike—just like that! She'd nearly died! I started my car. After he'd come in me, Mike had asked me whether I was on the pill. I'd said that there was no risk. He'd smiled; he thought it was wonderful.

He'd walked into my office the next morning. I was worried he wanted to talk about the day before. Sure enough, he did bring it up. Was I actually on the pill? I shook my head; I'd never said that. Mike was furious. I told him there was nothing to worry about, that he would just have to take my word for it. He came closer, clasped my face in his hands, and said I shouldn't mess with him. I said that I couldn't mess with him even if I wanted to.

He wondered why it had happened like that, so quickly, when we barely knew each other. I said I couldn't see the problem, it was on the cards—we'd worked together for a while, we saw each other every day. He asked me whether it was something I often did. I burst out laughing.

I switched to high beam; there was no one on the road.

I asked him if I looked like someone who would often do that. He shook his head—on the contrary. I confused him and that irritated him; he should have seen it from the start. I appeared to have the body of a smoker without being one. What did he mean, the body of a smoker? For the first time, we entered into a discussion that wasn't about work. Suppose we went on a date, he suggested. I didn't want to date. Suppose we go out to dinner? I didn't want to have dinner.

I'd have been happy to sleep with him again, but having dinner would be going too far.

An oncoming vehicle signalled me.

Quickly, I turned the high beam off.

Zanele told me she'd shown it to Shanla. I asked her what she was talking about.

The previous evening she had very carefully brought the bracelet out from under her bed. She had put it on, just for a moment. While she had it on, she had paraded around the room. Shanla had thought it was beautiful, and asked why she never wore it.

'And?' I asked.

'Too expensive,' she had replied.

I said I'd also like to see her with it on.

She smiled shyly.

'The colours are beautiful!'

'Yes, that red. That's what made me buy it for you. I told you what red meant, didn't I?'

Surprise coloured her face. Had I forgotten to tell her?

I didn't normally believe in superstitions, but I did have a thing about colours. I told her about the superstition some Jews had about red; not all Jews—there were those who used blue in the form of an eye. My grandmother had taught me to believe that you should always wear something red to protect you against the evil eye. It was absurd, of course, but the evil eye could be driven away by it. Zanele looked at me comprehendingly. She was familiar with the concept of the evil eye. And she knew it appeared in all tribes. She said she would wear it if it was needed. But to wear it every day would be a shame; it could break.

'But it won't just break. And if it breaks we'll fix it.'

'And if I lose?'

I frowned.

'You see? Kkkk.'

Zanele sliced the vegetables finely. There was something already standing on the stove, although I couldn't see what.

Out of the blue, while she continued chopping, she asked what the man's name had been.

'Wouter,' I answered. I was in the mood to tell her something, to talk to her. I was in the mood for women's talk. I leapt onto the bench, onto my spot, my feet resting on the rubbish bin.

She looked at me expectantly. This time it was I who was shy, and I let my eyelids drop. I stared at my hands lying in my lap. She tapped me and told me that she knew I'd had a great love, and she'd been waiting for me to start talking about it.

'Well, yes. Okay. It was the sort of love that you feel the whole day through.'

She became curious, just as she did when I told her about what I was reading. I had surprised myself with my silly answer. I sounded like a teenage girl.

She wanted to know how we had met each other. I'm not crazy about how-we-met stories, but I was glad she asked about it. I told her about my internship, how it had been at the hospital where he worked. She didn't know what an internship was. To learn, I repeated a couple of times, to learn on the job through practice. She nodded her head.

Wouter's expression had changed when he heard my surname. It turned out he knew my father—it was a small world, after all. A couple of students were allocated to work with senior doctors, and I was placed with him. I was immediately able to accompany him on his rounds and visit his patients. In between visits, he asked me questions with an intensity in his eyes that frightened me. There was something stern about him—very stern, but not threatening. He was the sort of man who seemed to have himself well under control, and that attracted me.

At the end of the third day we left the hospital at the same time. I had done my best to make sure this happened, hanging back in the hope we would leave together. It was only when I headed off with my bicycle in the direction of his car that I felt I had his attention.

He thought it was 'nice' that I was studying medicine, and 'nice' that he'd met me. I wanted to be more than the 'nice' daughter of Isaac Jinsky. His cold gaze intrigued me; I wanted to know what was behind it. Our clumsy conversation on the street became uncomfortable, but neither of us moved. Half leaning against his car, he said it was always bloody raining, except for now—he had no excuse for asking if I would leave my bike behind so he could drive me home.

I said I never left my bike behind anyway.

He shook his head exaggeratedly. I asked what was wrong.

'Cocky girls,' he said. 'What's a man to do with them?'

Zanele interrupted, asking why I hadn't brought my

bicycle with me.

'You couldn't cycle on these roads!'

'Maybe not. Okay, okay, and what did he look like?'

It was difficult to put into words. I told her how he'd shaved his head because he was quite bald. 'So the only colour in his face came from his lips and eyes. He had stern eyes. His nose was normal, not big, not small, and there was a very thin line running from the top of his nose that split his nostrils precisely in two. And he had a chin. What are you laughing at?'

'Everyone has chin!'

'No, I mean a strong chin. Like this.' I stretched my bottom lip and pushed my jaw forward. She stared at me, surprised. I obviously looked bizarre. 'It wasn't an ugly chin, but it gave his face a hard quality.'

'Okay, Joni, enough about face. Tell more! About him, with you!'

'I couldn't eat anything. I couldn't eat in front of him.'

She shook her head. 'Little girl!'

'He would sit staring at me the whole time. The first few times we went out together, you have no idea, I was sweating all over.'

'What?'

'Yes! Every time. I was soaked through, and it was still winter.'

She laughed out loud. Once she was silent again and had thrown the sliced vegetables in the boiling water, I saw she was still smiling. I could continue.

I told her about the student dorms—how, against the rules, he had a key for them; and how, late in the evenings, as soon as he could get away from home, he would come to me, sometimes in the middle of the night. 'We were just like teenagers!'

'Little girl,' she said again, and she tapped me on the leg.

'Yeah, you're right there, I was a girl. Or, rather, there was a girl in me ...'

I stared at the rubbish bin. 'That girl doesn't exist any more.'

'And the man? You still love the man?'

'Ach.'

Zanele turned the kettle on and made a cup of tea for me. I didn't want her to look after me; I wanted her to listen to me, to talk to me.

'It was difficult, Zanele. Like I said, he already had a family.'

'Excuses, always excuses!' she said, not knowing how right she was.

I leapt from the bench, walked to the fridge, and pulled the door open without wanting anything.

'Oohoo, easy, Joni!'

'Don't *easy* me!'

I slammed the fridge door shut, went over to the stove, and lifted the lid from a saucepan.

'Rice.'

'I can see that.' I was annoyed. Not with her, with me — for sitting there talking about myself, about things that bothered me. I should have stopped myself.

'Easy.'

I sighed, and watched as Zanele drained the rice and divided it between four plates — three of which would be served together.

Bloody hell, why was I eating on my own every evening?

She set three plates on a serving tray, and gave me the other.

Pieces of meat, vegetables, and rice.

She un-knotted her apron and pulled it off high over her head.

'Eat up, girlie.'

Everything was cut into small pieces, for Shanla. Not that she couldn't cut it herself, but she liked small things so much. And because I had once said it didn't matter to me, I too got everything in small pieces. All I needed was a fork. At a staccato pace, the fork stuffed the food into my mouth.

Did I still love him?

I wished I could never swallow another bite again. I wanted his eyes to be undressing me. I wanted to be getting warmer. I wanted him to be looking at me too long, as if he was making plans in his head that didn't concern me. And it didn't matter what I asked; he decided what I should hear. That drove me nuts. He drove me nuts. I thought about our nights, about never wanting to pee again, never wanting to wash myself again, and how I'd told him that after we'd made love. It had made him laugh, and he said I was sweet. He never knew I meant it, that in the morning I held my hand between my legs for ages so I could smell the previous evening on my fingers.

My fork went on tapping against an empty plate.

Zanele tried to get the house in order. It started in the hallway. She thought the folding chair by the front door was untidy, and moved it to a corner in the kitchen where, folded, it had no purpose whatsoever. By the front door I could always throw a bag or shawl onto it. Next she carried the huge stone statue out of the living room. 'Nice for hallway,' she said enthusiastically. After that, whenever I came home I was confronted at waist level by the eyes of a naked man.

The rest of the passage she left bare, and I had to let my bag fall on the cold stone floor. Then she would move it. I would find it under the staircase less than three metres away. It became a sort of ritual: throwing it down, shifting it, and picking it up again. Zanele thought the bag was more central under the stairs, and safer there than by the door, which we rarely walked past.

The house keys that I habitually left lying around received the same treatment. She had lived with me less than a week when she approached me with a grey tray. It looked like it was decorated with mosaic. I hadn't even known we had something that ugly in the house.

'For keys,' she said by way of announcement. With a flourish, she placed it on the flat head of the metre-high naked man. The days of throwing things down and leaving things lying around were over. I even had to be careful about how I placed my keys, otherwise the tray would slide from the statue's head onto the stone floor.

She never used the front door herself, but had her own entrance. The path connecting her room with the kitchen ran all the way to the front of the house, where it was closed off with a gate. Right next to the big wooden front door was a tall steel gate to which only she had the key. The house appeared to be built so that we could live together and still remain apart. Of course, it was ridiculous to live together and use different front doors. When I suggested to her that she should just use the wooden front door she started laughing out loud, and made it clear that it was out of the question. What sort of upbringing had I had, she asked jokingly.

There wasn't much to do in the living room. She didn't dare touch the CD player; the books she placed neatly back on the shelves—often upside down —after dusting them; and the CDs she piled just as I had myself. The wood that had been stacked next to the fireplace all year she put in a big bag, so that it looked tidier. The long-handled matches she put in the bookcase—something I only discovered, to my annoyance, after a long search the first evening that I wanted to light a fire. The fireplace provided our only heating. Every white house had one. I used it only when the stone floor felt really cold, two or three evenings a year. The rest of the winter evenings I wore extra layers of clothing.

She wasn't allowed to touch my desk. My piles of papers vexed her, as she didn't believe they were in any sort of order. She did dust the computer monitor regularly, which I could see in the mornings when the sun shone on it and warmed my back.

Once she removed a box of tablets from my desk. She looked concerned when she came to me with the box of Paludrine in her hand to ask what they were for. Were they very important, she asked; after all, the box had lain for ages next to my keyboard. I explained that I didn't take them any more; the box had been left on my desk from my last trip to a malaria zone. They didn't bother me there. Next to them was a glass jar full of vitamin tablets that I never touched. However, I did use the bottle of cognac that stood on the corner of my desk. I liked to have a sip or two when I was working in the evenings on a report. I'd tip my head back for a moment to feel the warmth stream down my throat, then I could see the poster hanging on the wall that I had pinched from outside the supermarket in the village. It showed a mother looking anxiously at a black teenage girl: 'I had sex, Mum. When will I die?'

A couple of days later, she'd moved the Paludrine to my bathroom. The pills lay there next to the right-hand washbasin, the one that was never used. Here they did bother me because they emphasised the fact that there was no one to use the washbasin.

But Zanele left the empty chewing-gum packets that were lying on my desk, and even the road atlas of South Africa that really belonged in the car.

Not much changed in my bedroom. She went upstairs at the end of each day to close the curtains — she thought I didn't do it neatly enough because I always left a slight gap through which bright light shone in the morning. She would fold down my bed and lay a clean t-shirt next to my pillow. Making my bed ready, as I called it. I didn't think it was necessary, but Zanele said she liked doing it.

My wardrobe, on the other hand, did look very different from how it had been before her arrival. Within a week she had sorted my clothes by colour. At first I thought she had just tidied up the cupboards, but then her system sank in. Gradually, I got used to her tidiness, and after a while I even started putting things back on my vanity unit in the right place of my own accord — the bottles kept separate from the tubes, and arranged by height.

After a long day at the hospital, I threw my bag down in the hall, and threw my keys into the tray atop the naked man. I heard Zanele in the kitchen, and went straight to her.

How had her day been, I asked. I hoisted myself up onto the bench, exhausted. I'd leapt up a hundred times before, but couldn't now.

She told me about her latest argument with Gibsan, the gardener of the Afrikaaners who lived a couple of metres further up our street. I barely knew the people. Occasionally, I'd seen them tear past in their *bakkie*, and then we'd greet each other. Their garden was clearly important to them, as Gibsan was there almost every day. It wasn't long before we'd claimed him as our handyman—not that we needed him often. I took after my mother, who used to have the plumber repairing bicycle punctures, and the window-washer painting the house. Usually, I fixed things myself, but ever since the blockage in the bathroom Gibsan had helped us.

It had been Zanele's idea to ask for his help, and he had succeeded in getting the washbasin to drain freely again. He thought it had something to do with calcium build-up. Not that he knew the word for it, but what he showed us looked damned like calcium. Later, our washing machine gave up the ghost, and we had to wait until Gibsan, together with some vague acquaintances of his, had time to come and repair it. In the meantime, we took our washing to the laundry.

When I said to Zanele that she and Gibsan had an impressive love-hate relationship, she was furious. As if!

'You have an argument every day! If it were otherwise you'd stay away from each other.'

She said it was all his fault. He wouldn't leave her alone;

he wanted to know everything about her. That I could believe. How often had I arrived home only to find him waiting, coincidentally, at our gate? He would look searchingly at me. When Zanele was annoyed with him, she called him 'noseyparker'; otherwise, she called him 'blackie'. The first time I heard her say this I asked her why on earth she called him that.

'He is very black!'

'Look who's talking!'

She laughed, and said he was much blacker than she was. She was right there. She explained that you could see from the darkness of someone's skin how far north they had been born, relative to here. The further north, the darker, she said. Gibsan came from Malawi, and had been here a couple of years. He had come on foot, and that was a long way.

I asked what the argument was about this time.

She had wanted to borrow his scissors.

'You see. You sought him out!'

She pushed her whole body against me. I clung to the bench top.

'And he asked about you, but none of his business.' She knotted her apron tighter behind her back. I asked what on earth he wanted to know.

She didn't answer. She just smoothed the apron across her belly.

Why didn't she answer me? Because it was personal? Had he asked why I lived alone?

'Did he want to know why I don't have a husband?'

She went on with her cooking with an air of exaggerated concentration. So I was on the right track. I couldn't be bothered with this today. It was none of Gibsan's business.

She was still ignoring my question, but it was a topic she herself sometimes brought up. I leapt from the bench to break the silence. I did it too quickly, and the rubbish bin fell over. Simultaneously, we bent to pick it up. Rubbish had fallen out.

'I'll do it, leave it,' she said, irritated, as we picked up the mess. But it was my fault. And my rubbish bin.

Only after we had shut the lid did she say that that wasn't what Gibsan had asked.

'Pretty young woman, no children. Seems strange to him.'

She looked at me a second too long before walking to the kitchen sink to wash her hands. I waited. After she had dried her hands she gestured that it was my turn. I rinsed my hands with water and soap. I was sweating.

She stood directly in front of me and gave me a tea towel. Then she walked to the cupboard and took out one glass. I made room in front of the sink. Zanele turned on the tap, waited until the water was cold, and filled the glass, which she then pressed into my hands. I hadn't asked for it, and she hadn't asked if I wanted it. She just pressed it into my hands. I wasn't thirsty. When I folded my hands around it, I could feel the slackness of my fingers.

'Just drink some.'

I didn't respond. Her face came closer. That could mean one of two things: she hadn't understood me or I should listen better.

Without having had a sip, I placed the glass down on the bench. I didn't like mains water.

She turned back to the stove. 'Kkkk.'

Burnt pans were a feature of her cooking.

The point of Zanele's blue woollen beanie stuck out of her cardigan pocket. That way, she could pull it out at any moment. She was going on about close weather and low clouds. Today was the day. I looked at her questioningly. It was warm, yes, just like other days, with some low-lying clouds. I nodded.

'Sun hidden.'

I nodded again. The sun had no rights today.

The stifling air pressed inside through the kitchen door. Had I finished my work, she asked.

I had finished all the reports from the previous day, except for the last two. I indicated that it was more or less taken care of. She smiled. So was this a good day to finally go to the hairdresser? She had tried every week to get me there. She didn't care for the fact that I trimmed my own fringe.

I fell in with her plans.

She directed me to a village that I'd never been to before. After we had parked, we walked for a while through small, busy streets full of people hanging about and gossiping. Zanele was greeted by quite a few people along the way, although I couldn't tell how well they knew her. No one greeted me.

I wondered what I was in for when we went into some sort of hair salon where I was immediately put in a chair. Afrikaans or English, asked the hairdresser; it didn't matter to her. It was never a good sign if it didn't matter. I began to explain what I wanted in Afrikaans: everything shorter, but my fringe mustn't be too short; it should hang just above my eyebrows so I could retreat behind it when I wanted. Zanele asked again if I didn't want to be rid of the fringe altogether—it looked so childish. I said I was leaving.

'Okay, okay. *Easy*, Joni.'

With wet hair, I was seated once again in the chair. The hairdresser said something to Zanele in Zulu that she thought I wouldn't understand.

This was the first time she'd cut straight hair.

I felt even more anxious. I looked in the mirror at my straight black hair—my hairdo. I'd always been someone with a hairdo. I focused on the scissors while Zanele gossiped with the hairdresser from the chair next to mine. The undercurrent of Zulu annoyed me; I thought it was impolite, although Zanele had often told me I should be more understanding.

I paid the bill of ten rand, and had to admit she had done a good job. I asked Zanele whether she would also like a haircut. Shocked, she shook her head. I rearranged a couple of hairs and, satisfied, we left the salon. Zanele tapped my arm on the way to the car. 'You see!' We decided to make it a regular appointment.

'But then also for you,' I suggested.

'You're out of your mind!'

I was never sure whether she was pulling my leg when she parroted me like that, or whether she had only half-remembered a remark. I had to laugh. At the same time, I remembered that every year at the first real heat she cut her hair short all over, as short as a man's, and that nothing more needed to be done to it.

When we arrived home, Zanele got out while the motor was still running; I had to go straight on to the hospital. It was quiet on the roads. I would be just in time.

A badly wounded youth was being brought in as I arrived. That had never happened to me before, not at the exact same second. I ran to the department to get ready as quickly as possible. I wasn't sure what had happened to him, but the seriousness of the situation was obvious. His face was so badly damaged I had difficulty looking at him, especially at his left eye, which wouldn't be able to be saved. That looked as if it was the first injury he had sustained, and his eye socket was empty. It was only after, that I saw all the bullet wounds in his muscular torso. His bleeding heart just kept pumping, and the blood was sloshing from his body. Albert raced to the surgeons who, after a short discussion, agreed to give it a go.

At the end of the afternoon I decided to visit Mike and find out how it had gone with the wounded Xhosa boy. I hadn't heard anything over the course of the day. That wasn't unusual, as it was always insane in our area.

There was a strange atmosphere in his department. I hurried to his office and knocked on the door while simultaneously pulling it open. Mike sat slumped in his desk chair, his attention on a superball. He wasn't expecting me. He straightened his back and set the ball down on his desk, and it immediately rolled off. As he was bending over to pick it up, he broke the news that the operation had been too taxing for the patient; there hadn't been anything they could do. Now upright, he looked at me. 'Such a young man, such a strong body …'

I nodded. It was what I had noticed, too. Mike told me he was broken up by it. I said it went with the territory, with the job. He started talking about fate.

I said I had no patience with complaints about fate. Fate

was life, that's what I had been taught.

It took a while for my words to sink in. He didn't respond. The yellow ball bounced twice, his eyes locked on it. For the first time he didn't look directly at me, even though there was only the two of us. That happens after a death, I thought. I thanked him for the news.

Why was I so cold, he asked, just as my right hand grasped the door handle.

I froze. 'Excuse me?'

He inclined his head a little to the right, and from where I stood appeared to be inspecting me. I folded my arms over each other so that I felt less exposed. While he rolled the ball in his right hand, he went on looking searchingly at my upper body as if my arms weren't there. I felt an excitement I hadn't been prepared for. His eyes began to compel me as they had the previous time.

I'd gladly have gone back for more.

After two weeks of working fourteen days straight, I had a whole day off. Not that I could see the point of it, but I had a day off.

I heard someone walking along the upstairs passage as I was getting dressed. From the speed of the footsteps, it sounded like Shanla. My jeans were already buttoned, and I quickly pulled a shirt over my head.

Shanla's glass jar was in her right hand; she said she wanted to show me something. When she came nearer, I could see that she had caught some horrible thing. With a smile even broader than normal, she pushed the glass jar close to my face.

'Go away, Shanla!'

She laughed loudly and told me that the insect had been silly enough to fly onto our path. I could see something that looked like a cross between a bee and a spider, or at least it had the torso of a bee with the legs of a spider. It was repulsive! I didn't want to be reminded of all the insects that lived here; the insects in this country scared me more than the carnivores did.

'What will you do with it?' I asked. It wasn't even seven o'clock in the morning and she'd already got the day's catch. She wanted to show it to Gibsan. She explained that this insect usually walked along the ground, in the sand, and rarely flew. Because it so rarely flew it was a bad flyer, and hence easy to catch.

I remarked that it actually looked a bit like a bee.

'A bee?' She began shaking her head to indicate that I had it all wrong.

'Bees make honey. This stupid spider can't do anything!'

She peered into her glass jar where the bee-spider was crawling rather than flying.

'Look,' she said. 'He's even got sand on his feet.'

There were maybe two sand grains visible; they looked more like dust. Just dust, like everything is made of here.

I asked her whether she knew why everything was always so dusty. Personally, I thought it was because of the roads: they were unmade, so every passing car threw up clouds of dust. You rarely saw asphalt here.

After a short pause, she said it was because of the wind. Because the wind blew so little, the dust couldn't blow away—her mother had once explained it to her. She put on the same serious face as when she was reading.

I looked at her with raised eyebrows. 'Doesn't the wind just make it worse?'

She shook her head.

'Joni?'

'Yes?'

'What is the difference between sand and dust?'

I was silent for a moment. 'Sand comes from the sea.' She watched me, interested. 'The land is made of sand; you can see that here because there are so many unpaved areas, like the big deserts. You can also see it if you're at the beach.'

From her expression, I could tell she'd never been to a beach.

'Whereas dust is made from dry bits of lots of different things. We just call them all dust, a collective name. Dust moves easily and blows away easily.'

She was probably wondering to herself what role the wind played. She went on looking at me seriously.

I asked if the lid was on her jar properly, otherwise the filthy creature would be buzzing loose through the house. She nodded. I walked to the stairs.

'Everything is sand,' she mumbled.

And dust, I thought. I wondered if I had explained it all properly, or had I only confused her? I wanted to take her to the Cape so that she could see the beach. There, I would let her feel the power of the sea without letting go of her for more than a second. Zanele would be waiting for us back on the beach with our towels unfolded.

When we arrived downstairs, Zanele asked me if we could do the shopping in my car, since I had a day off. It would save her walking in the heat. I suggested we go early to the village, straight away.

A quarter of an hour later she got into the car with bare feet. Wasn't she going to put her shoes on, I asked, gesturing towards the pair she held in her hand. She shook her head. She hated shoes.

Shanla stayed behind, playing under the big tree on the corner. Still holding the glass jar, she was there with Happy's daughter. Happy worked for our Afrikaans neighbours. I couldn't see whether the girls had already set the insect free. Shanla called out something as we left. I shook my head and Zanele agreed with me; ice cream was out of the question.

A bit further along, Mbufu was lying in the grass. It was only when he waved to us that you could see he was awake. Beside him lay lots of light-green tendrils that must have been from an eaten corn-cob. The cob itself he had probably thrown away. For the umpteenth time, Zanele told me how he couldn't find any work—because he wasn't capable of anything and because there weren't any jobs. I offered to see if there was a job going in the laundry back at the hospital. She doubted whether he'd be able to do it.

'Why do you always put him down?'

She wound her window down for the breeze. I was the one sweating, not her. Zanele was always dry. She didn't answer my question.

I asked her to get my sunglasses from the glove box. Behind the wheel, with my sunglasses on, I felt just like my mother.

Had I told Zanele about the first time I'd been to the supermarket here? She didn't know the story, as it had happened before she came to live with me. Since then, I'd rarely been back. I told her how the black cashier had told me off when I went to pay. I had chosen between four sorts of sugar, none of which were known to me, but the one I'd bought wasn't used by whites. The cashier had asked me whether I wanted to swap it. 'Sugar is sugar,' I'd said.

Zanele had to laugh—she knew exactly which brand I had taken. 'Our new apartheid!' she hooted. We were stationary for a moment at an intersection. A fat blowfly flew into the car. Zanele began to swat at it. She swore every time she missed. And then suddenly she was holding the palm of her hand right in front of my face.

'Get off. Take it away!'

She examined the tiny corpse, and remarked that she'd broken off a leg. I felt nauseous, and said that now I understood where Shanla's gory interest in insects had come from. She laughed proudly.

Had I noticed, she asked, that flies always flew the same way, repeatedly crashing against the same windows without finding a way out? If she hadn't killed it, it would never have left the car. She sounded like she knew what she was talking about.

'Like whiteys in township—don't come out, not alive,' she said, as she threw her catch out the window. And just like every other time the topic of townships came up, she started warning me never to take the wrong turn-off by accident, and always to pay attention on the roads.

Had she already thought of what we needed from the supermarket, I asked. I didn't feel like walking around there for hours.

She patted me. '*Easy.*'

Just as I'd expected, we walked around Pick'n Pay for more than an hour.

At the lolly section I asked her what Shanla liked, and without looking Zanele pointed to the acid drops. She was distracted by two men near us. I turned around, and now I saw what she was looking at. They had taken a bag of chips and were quickly eating them. We exchanged glances without saying anything. With two packets of acid drops in our trolley, we walked on.

She asked if I knew what blacks called this supermarket.

I shook my head.

'Pick no pay.'

I burst out laughing.

'Everyone says it—everyone!'

She pointed to the freezer full of chicken. 'That's all.' Mbufu's father had apparently never wanted anything else. I asked when Mbufu was going to visit his father again, but it appeared not to be on the cards. The last time, he hadn't been given a cent.

When we finally arrived at the queue in front of the cash register, she said she'd go and stand on the other side to pack everything in bags.

'No way, we'll do it together.'

'Kkkk.'

I clicked back. For the first time.

Zanele tapped me. She mimicked me and I her. We went on mimicking each other, louder and louder. Everyone stared. I couldn't have cared less, but Zanele did. A woman caught her eye and she immediately fell silent. I asked what was wrong. She tapped her lips with her index finger.

On the return trip, we stopped at the mail-boxes to see if there was anything for us. I didn't see the point, as we never received any mail. I waited at the corner while Zanele slowly stepped out. Her tempo never changed. She took the key from her pocket and opened the mail-box. I could see it was empty. She closed the box again and gave it a tap before she came back, shaking her head to and fro. 'No mail, Joni.'

To drive out of the village you had to drive back past the supermarket.

Pick no pay.

Shanla ran towards us with some sort of flute in her hand: a wooden stick with a couple of holes in it. Gibsan had given it to her, though she didn't know how he came to have it. She held it close to her face with her two hands. I asked her if she'd tried it yet.

'Not myself,' she said. But Gibsan had showed her how to do it. I said it was no good just to sit and watch. She put the flute carefully to her mouth and began to blow. There was barely any sound coming out. She went and sat on the ground and blew, enthralled.

Zanele unloaded the groceries, and I decided to do some work on a file. I grabbed the last one from the day before, an unclear case. We were waiting for blood-test results; the patient probably just had Aids.

A couple of hours later, I heard Shanla playing three notes in succession. I watched her and her flute through the big kitchen window. Suddenly, I was reminded of my first opera and how carefully I'd dressed up for it. Oma Anna had talked to me about the opera, and we had listened to the music for weeks beforehand to make it more meaningful. I had to pay attention to the details, the trilogy, and the number three — the sign of the Freemasons. And the Temple of Wisdom — she'd talked about that a lot. I remembered how we'd entered the opera arm-in-arm, and how grown up it had made me feel.

When Shanla noticed me, she stopped playing. She held the flute in her hand and stood in the doorway.

The kitchen had two doors. Usually, Zanele left the back door standing open the whole day so she could hear Shanla playing on the path. Sometimes, if she had to do something elsewhere in the house, she would lock the big steel gate so she could leave the other kitchen door open. This way she could also hear Gibsan if he stood, shirtless, calling from the gate.

'Reading is more fun,' Shanla said.

Could we read together?

I nodded; after all, it was my day off.

I'd never sat so long on the path as I did that afternoon. Shanla stood up after we'd been reading for three-quarters of an hour and started doing all sorts of dances. Her bare feet were used to the paving stones. She knew so many different steps and wanted me to see them all. Some were just hopping; others, she'd obviously learnt from someone. She moved like a dance girl. I watched her closely. Her legs looked skinny — they were long in comparison to the rest of her body, which still didn't have much shape, although she already had two small bumps on her chest.

The department was in a panic. When I came in, I immediately went looking for Albert. His assistant told me he wasn't there. But wasn't he on shift?

Our ambulance had been stolen.

'Stolen?' Where was Albert then?

She explained that he'd left for the police station as soon as he'd heard. This was a serious matter.

But why would anyone want an ambulance? Surely it would be easily recognised. Albert's assistant explained that it would be quickly re-sprayed in the township — they would get more for it than if they'd just stolen a car. Now they had a car, as well as the equipment, tools, and all the other things they'd find on board.

At first, I thought the robbery had happened here, in the grounds, but then I heard that our driver had been behind the wheel and that Steve, one of the nurses, had been with him. Now I understood why there was such a sense of panic.

In the meantime, Albert had been a long time at the station. Our two colleagues would have resisted, of course; they had to be found. The sooner the better. Both Thabi and Steve had worked with us for years. Thabi was black. Would that make any difference?

The assistant shook her head.

I suggested we get on with our work; there were patients enough. On the way to the department's first room, the assistant told me how it had been a normal ambulance call. They had left with only two men as there weren't enough personnel. It happened more and more these days. Usually, it was a question of just loading the ambulance and getting back to the hospital as quickly as possible. According to the assistant, it was just as well there hadn't been a third person: 'If they're capable of this, they'll cut three throats just as easily as two.'

I immediately felt nauseous. I saw Steve and Thabi tied to tree trunks with their throats slit, all for a stupid truck. How was it possible that we hadn't anticipated this — that it had been so easy to trick us, to get the ambulance into a bad neighbourhood? The ambulance staff had to be armed; this mustn't be allowed to happen again.

Albert came back a couple of hours later. There were still no reports, no trace of them. He looked wretched. He didn't want to dwell on it any further.

We never spoke of it again until the day he was called away to identify Steve, about a week later. Could I work late, as he had to go down to the station? Of course, I said. At the same time I took the opportunity to ask whether in the future we should arm the ambulance staff. With or without permission.

Albert shook his head. 'We're not cowboys.'

I raised my eyebrows. 'If you're surrounded by cowboys you'll lose all your horses.'

He looked at me full of contempt.

Did this country have to end up like the rest of the continent, he asked.

Maybe, I thought. Maybe the God of Africa is a cowboy.

After the lights in my study had caused the fuse to blow several times, I asked Gibsan whether he knew an electrician. He would arrange one. He couldn't say when they would turn up, but he would do his best. That same evening there was a loud knock on the front door, about half an hour after we had eaten and Zanele had said goodnight. Someone yelled in Zulu that he had been sent by Gibsan to look at the lights.

I opened the door and there stood a man in shorts, without any tools. He was sorry, he said, he only spoke Zulu. We'd figure it out, I answered. Even so, I decided to get Zanele so we could better explain what was wrong with the lights. Could he wait a moment?

I hurried along the path to Zanele's room and knocked on her door. I could hear water running, but there was no answer. She probably hadn't heard me. Carefully, I opened the door to the room. Out of the corner of my eye I saw Mbufu standing under the shower. There was no one else there. I took a step backwards, but I was too slow; he'd already seen me. I immediately apologised.

Mbufu opened his mouth and let the water stream in. His penis caught my eye. I couldn't look away. He asked what I was there for.

'Where's your mother? I need some help with Zulu,' I stuttered.

She had just gone to visit Happy, further up the road.

Could he help me? He had never sounded so helpful, but then we had never really had a conversation before, and certainly not when he was naked.

'No, don't worry, don't rush, I'll try and do it myself.' I felt like saying he had a fabulous body.

Mbufu nodded and turned around. I stayed looking a fraction too long before I walked from the room.

The electrician was still standing motionless in the hall.

'Would you like to come this way?'

While I tried to explain where I had the short circuit, without knowing the word for short circuit, the image of Mbufu remained in my mind. I realised I'd never done it with a black man, even though I'd been here for years and 90 per cent of the population was black.

From the vacant look on his face, I realised the man didn't know anything about lighting or electricity. He just stood aimlessly looking around. After a short silence, he said he couldn't see what the problem was. The only thing he could think of was that I needed a new light.

I was so sick of that after all these years; every time something was broken you had to replace it—repairs weren't even considered. Car wrecks lined the roads. I had even accused Zanele of being too quick to say something had to be thrown away when it wasn't justified. I sighed and thanked the man for coming. Had he come far? He shook his head. His nephew was a friend of the boy who worked on the corner of the street, at the first house, and he had asked him during the afternoon, on behalf of Gibsan, if he could drop by.

Was he an electrician by profession, I asked.

No, he worked as a farm labourer, the first half of every week.

Thanks for nothing, Gibsan.

I asked him whether I owed him anything.

He said he would like a Coca-Cola, if I had any in the house. I gave him a bottle to take with him. After an exaggerated bow, he turned away. Unscrewing the cap of the bottle, he slowly left my house. I collapsed on the couch. I would have to get someone else to look at the lighting in my study.

A knock at the kitchen door startled me. It must be Zanele, who'd heard I'd been to her place. I yelled that she could come in.

Mbufu was standing there. I sat up straight, and couldn't help casting a glance at his crotch again, even though he was now wearing pants.

He asked whether it had been fixed.

'Not really. Gibsan sent a farm labourer to look at my lights.'

Mbufu laughed and looked around him. In his black English, he said he rarely came in here; he had no reason to. 'Will you stay awhile?' I asked.

He didn't answer.

I asked why he spoke so little Afrikaans. He told me that he had grown up in a different area from Shanla. That was why he didn't like talking. Had I never noticed? I smiled.

Of course, speaking Zulu with his mother and sister and the people in the street didn't help his Afrikaans, either. Was that why he couldn't find any work?

Mbufu smiled. 'Dust.'

He pointed with his finger to his head and repeated with a mocking glance, 'Dust.'

'Dust?'

'Yeah, you know, dust, like on road.'

I nodded, but couldn't see where the idea came from.

'Is what my mom say.'

It became clearer.

'But no true. Is no jobs, that's it.'

That sounded more like it. How could Zanele say something like that to her own son? A head full of dust? How denigrating could she be?

I said that indeed there wasn't much work. He obviously knew nothing about the offer I'd once made to his mother, to see whether I could find work for him at the hospital. His black eyes had lit up momentarily, but after this initial interest he fell back into despondency. It didn't appeal to him travelling so far every day. And what would he be able to do there? He'd never been to school.

I apologised again for bursting in on him. He said it didn't matter; his sister often stood watching when he had a shower. I didn't understand why they didn't have a curtain.

I tried to bring the discussion back to work.

He was no longer Zanele's son, but a seventeen-year-old man.

Once, when we'd driven past, from a distance she'd pointed out her old neighbourhood, roughly half an hour from here. Other than the suburb and the name of her former 'Madam', Brenda, I knew almost nothing about her previous work situation. She had apparently worked there a long time.

'Real Afrikaaners.' She was slicing the chicken into tiny pieces.

'That could mean anything!' She could mean that they were real racists, or real farmers. Or real racist farmers.

No, they weren't racist, but Madam Brenda obviously had problems with blacks. 'Trauma,' added Zanele proudly. She said the word just as I had taught her. We'd once practised a lot on the 'au'.

'What sort of trauma?' I asked her.

Zanele stopped slicing and looked at me. She wiped her right hand on her apron.

One Sunday morning, Madam Brenda had been walking to church with her nine-year-old daughter. They were less than two minutes from home when the girl realised she'd forgotten her hat. It was too hot to be walking without a hat. She went back to get it. In those two minutes she was taken by farm labourers—in that very small village where, during the apartheid years, it had been safe to walk around.

Madam Brenda couldn't understand why going to get a hat was taking her so long. A quarter of an hour later she came across her daughter, covered in blood. Her only child. After that they had moved, to Gauteng.

'Madam Brenda said nothing. I know from her husband, when I asked why my boyfriend couldn't come, only girlfriends.'

Zanele went back to work. She threw the rice from the big packet into a pan of boiling water. Alcohol is at the bottom of these things, she went on to say. The whites are responsible. This was one of her theories. Certainly it was true in the Cape area, she said, where Madam Brenda came from, where there are so many wine regions and where the employees, the farm labourers, were paid with alcohol.

I didn't believe it. Wouldn't they still need cash for their families?

'Right,' said Zanele. But the cash only made up a small part of their pay.

Which was all to the good, anyway. After a while, the men only ended up addicted and then they would spend all the money on drink.

'What vegetables are you cooking?'

'*Mielies*,' she said, with a grin and raised brows. Personally, she was crazy about corn.

One way or another, you heard stories like the one about

Brenda's daughter so often that you soon became desensitised to them. At first, a story like that would have haunted me for hours, and I would picture what it must have been like for a nine-year-old girl. Until I made myself sick. The longer I lived here the less sensitive I'd become. I, too, buried myself in all the current theories, in the underlying thoughts and explanations. But I doubted if alcohol was the only culprit.

'How long did you work there?'

She had to think about it, and began to count out loud. It had been dull, she said.

'Why?'

She shrugged her shoulders—a movement that rendered her body unusually dull.

'Madam didn't speak,' she said, while she turned the chicken in the oil.

A couple of minutes later, Zanele walked to the sink with the hot vegetable pan, held the lid against it, and allowed the water and froth to run out.

Couldn't we just buy a colander, I asked.

'Don't need, this is fine,' she said, her back turned toward me, absorbed, bent over the sink. I shuffled a bit further towards the back of the bench.

She cooked a lot more corn than we could eat. She always did, simultaneously preparing the lunch for the following day. One corn-cob per person was just right. The cobs served as a meal. What happened with the husks didn't matter; you found the pale green threads everywhere on the streets.

Could I move my legs from off the bench, asked Zanele. I was sitting at some distance from the food, so I couldn't see why. I let them fall back onto the rubbish bin.

Once the cobs were well cooked, she peeled one. Carefully, she sliced the corn off the cob, and the grains fell straight onto the plate. I was the only one in the house who didn't gnaw the cob. I'd tried it a couple of times early on, but hated the threads that got stuck between my teeth.

'Your teeth aren't made for it,' she said, as if a white person's teeth couldn't gnaw.

I was on the way upstairs, half reading. I bumped into Zanele coming down the stairs with the pedal bin from the bathroom in her hands.

'Sorry.'

She said it didn't matter, and walked on through to my study. I knew her route: via my study, where she collected the wastepaper bin, to the kitchen, where she threw all the household rubbish together and prepared it for the neighbourhood collection-point. The closest collection-point was quite a few streets away. Gibsan transported our garbage bags there — she'd arranged that well.

It seemed he did it for the other three houses in the street as well; only for Zanele, he charged nothing. He used to pick up the bags in a trailer, as they were too heavy to carry. More than that, the distance between the four houses was quite big. I had once explained to Zanele that in the Netherlands a street this long would have thirty houses on it. She'd just shrugged her shoulders.

The collection-point was emptied almost every week, although on arbitrary days. The stinking air greeted you as you approached. Whether your car windows were open or shut made no difference. The other distinguishing feature of the place was the number of boys hanging around. Once, when we passed one of these 'hanging-out tips', Zanele had told me about the deals made there. Canny youths knew how to make something from them. Not Mbufu. He'd never produced anything—she despaired of him. To make it clear that she herself had done her best for him, she started telling me about the 'rubber weeks' she'd arranged for him. He would come home in the evenings with the same amount of rubber she'd sent him off with in the mornings. After three rubber weeks, Mbufu had started biting his nails. Zanele pulled a face. It was one of the things that really irritated her. Like his cap—the cap that was too small for him but that he refused to take off.

'It leaves ugly stripe here,' she said, drawing a horizontal line with her index finger above her eyebrows. Then she shook her head, as if to shake off the mark and her irritation.

'Nonsense, Zanele. I've seen him without his cap. He doesn't have any mark at all!'

'No, you can't see it, is still black!'

In the kitchen she threw the small rubbish bags together into the larger one. I came to get a drink. I pretended not to have seen her so I wouldn't interrupt.

'Joni?'

With raised brows, I turned to face her.

'Is odd, and I wonder about it since living here, but didn't dare ask.'

'What is it?'

She looked straight at me. 'Is never pads.'

Pads?

I didn't understand her.

'In here,' she said, with the bathroom pedal bin in her hand.

I looked at her questioningly.

'Or anything else, for monthlies.'

It would never have occurred to me that someone would concern themselves with the contents of a waste bin. Is that what happened when you had to empty them? Did you develop a sudden interest in the contents? It wasn't like her to make me feel so uncomfortable. Evidently, she'd been brooding about it for ages.

I felt caught out, caught out by something that just wasn't there. An absence had betrayed me. I turned away so she couldn't see me blush. How should I respond?

I stared at the white-tiled floor. I could understand it if she'd come across something strange, something she'd never seen before. I couldn't hear her moving. She was probably still standing there with the pedal bin in her hand, waiting for my answer. I stared at the floor; slowly the lines between the tiles vanished. One big white surface.

She had decided not to move until I'd answered. 'Could you just shut the lid first?' I asked, irritated. She immediately let it fall shut.

She looked at me sternly, as if to let me know it was a serious matter that had happened to come to light in the context of the rubbish.

I was behaving just like my mother had when she refused to respond to my father's comments.

'Why don't you answer?' Zanele asked.

My father had asked the same thing when he couldn't stand it any longer. I remembered my mother's standard reply, and began to smile. 'Because you haven't asked a question.'

Zanele was not to be fobbed off so easily.

'Okay then. Why is never pads in waste bin, how can that be?'

She remained patient; she stood straight and waited once again. This time, she knew she could count on an answer.

'You mean ...' I said, my voice breaking.

She nodded quickly, and too often, to make it clear that was what she meant.

'I don't use any pads.'

'Yeah, I know, but also nothing else. Is not possible'

I looked straight at her and swallowed. 'I don't bleed, Zanele.'

'Eh?'

I pressed my lips together. Her posture had immediately changed, and she seemed not to be standing as straight as she moved her head, which was now tilted to one side, towards me. She always moved closer when there was something she didn't understand.

Her eyes glanced over my body in order to reassure herself that I was as young as I looked—that it was nothing to do with my age. She frowned. 'You're young.'

Silence fell. I couldn't utter a word.

She just stood there looking at me. 'Sorry for questions, Joni. Sorry ...'

I walked out of the kitchen without taking a sip of my water. All at once, the familiar sense of hopelessness overwhelmed me. There was an emptiness in my head and simultaneously in my belly. I shut the door of my study, which I hardly ever did, let myself fall into my chair, and felt the hate welling up all over again.

I shook my head. I mustn't blame her.

Since that afternoon at my parent's house, the afternoon on which I became aware of what was wrong with me, and realised what my mother had done to me by never telling me what she'd taken, since that one afternoon I couldn't help but hold her responsible. My mother realised the seriousness of the situation, and avoided all eye-contact. She started talking about my father, how together they'd decided not to say anything about it. Could I forgive her?

But then who should I blame?

She offered to help me. I said she could help me by staying away. I rushed to the front door, out of their house. I'd pull my jacket on outside, on my bike. She ran after me.

She called out to me, but I was already gone.

I had to speak to Wouter. I wanted to ask him so much. Was this the explanation he was looking for? And other things, completely different things. Would he have left his family if he had known this? Suddenly, I started sweating. Would he stay with me?

My legs wouldn't pedal any faster. It was as if time no longer mattered. As if I could leave it at that.

Zanele knocked loudly because of the shut door. I asked what she wanted. She opened the door, and I saw her standing there with the wastepaper basket in her hands. It was a poor excuse. She couldn't meet my eyes.

My face was buried in my hands. Even now, I could feel the sweat breaking out under my fringe. My elbows rested on my knees close to my crossed feet. It was lucky my desk chair didn't have any armrests. With a quick wipe I dried my forehead. She asked if I was okay. I nodded and tried to smile.

She couldn't forget the incident. I could see it in her behaviour in the days that followed. She was uncomfortable; it had confused her. Still, she knew better than to pursue it, and she didn't ask about it again. Not even two days later when we were going to the laundromat.

On the way she told me about the owner—she'd heard that the laundromat and the drying shop belonged to the same man. I asked her who'd told her. She'd heard it from another housekeeper who had been waiting in the queue with her on the previous visit. It surprised me, as there were a couple of streets between the two businesses. Why hadn't he combined them?

The first time Zanele had mentioned the drying shop, I didn't know what she was talking about. Since then, I'd been there with her every summer. The drying shop operated only in the summer, while the laundromat was busy all year. We always saw acquaintances of Zanele's there. After she had greeted someone she'd tell me who it was, how they knew each other, and what they had to do with one another—which was usually nothing.

When we'd seen certain people a couple of times, people who never said hello to me, I knew as much about them as Zanele. Why these people didn't greet me wasn't clear to me. The stupid thing was, I would go on nodding and smiling, without getting any response. I asked Zanele if that ever happened to her. She said no.

Whenever we saw Charlotta, I thought of white tigers. Charlotta was a black woman without pigment. She looked different. She stood out due to her strange colour: she had all the hallmarks of a black woman, without being one. The first time Zanele pointed Charlotta out to me I called her an albino, but Zanele didn't know the word. She already had a nickname she'd said—she was called the white tiger. She had no camouflage. She had always been unique in her township. And like albinos in the townships, white tigers were rare in the wild.

'White tigers are very vulnerable,' I said to Zanele when she'd told me about Charlotta's nickname. I suggested the nickname wasn't quite right. Zanele agreed with me on that. 'We can see she is one of us.'

Zanele and Gibsan were sitting under the big tree on the corner. Zanele's teeth flashed—not because I'd pulled up, but obviously at something Gibsan had said.

Twenty minutes later, I heard the kitchen door creaking. She came into my study in bare feet, a banana in her hands. She thought it would be a good idea if I ate it. I had probably not eaten again? I agreed, and asked her what Gibsan had had to say. She immediately started laughing. The Minister of Safety's son had been picked up.

'Murder?'

'No, thief!' she roared. She thought it was fantastic. And he was still in custody. Thirteen thousand rand had to be paid for his release. Blackie knew all the details.

I shook my head.

'Why not funny?'

I shrugged my shoulders. 'It's sad, Zanele, surely?'

She thought I was over-reacting; it was only right that the boy had made his own father look a fool.

'But he makes the whole country look a fool.'

She curled her lips and looked at me searchingly.

'The sweater, Joni, the sweater. Take off!'

It was about thirty degrees and I was wearing a polo-neck sweater. I was cold. Her head signalled towards the garden—she suggested I go outside for once. Sitting inside the whole time was pathetic.

She walked to the big sliding door in my study and pulled it wide open. 'Come on!'

I left the half-eaten banana on my desk and got up.

Outside, my sweater was far too warm after all. It was usually quite fresh in the hospital, I ventured. She gave me a push. 'Kkkk!'

I let myself fall full-length on the grass, stretched, and lay there. It looked as if leaves were falling from the trees, but instead of falling they were twisting in the air. Some moved upwards, even though there was no wind. Come to think of it, they weren't even the colour of leaves: they were a cream colour.

It was only then I noticed that there weren't any bare trees—everything was still in full bloom. They were butterflies. With half-closed eyes I looked upwards to Zanele, who stood on the grass in the bright sunlight.

'So many butterflies!'

She nodded. 'Is butterfly month,' she said with a smile. It was the middle of November, spring had started only three days ago, and now it was already summer. I pulled my polo neck over my head and sat on the grass in my bra. Zanele came and stood in front of me, bent over as if to block someone's view—someone who mustn't see my uncovered upper body.

I pushed my fringe back where it belonged. 'There is no one here. What does it matter?'

She said she would run and get a shirt.

Slowly, she walked from the garden, through the open sliding door of the study on her way upstairs. There was no point in arguing with her. Once she had an idea in her head, there was no stopping her. But I didn't want a shirt; I wanted to feel butterflies against my skin.

In my rear-vision mirror I could see the sun sinking below the hills. Within a few minutes it would be pitch black, and I still had a fair way to go before home. For the first time, I realised that it made no sense to live almost an hour from the hospital. Maybe I should move after all. I didn't belong anywhere, so I could live anywhere. On the other hand, I liked the seemingly endless road, as well as the clouds of dust the car threw up behind it. I couldn't have cared less about the house, even though we had been living there for a couple of years. I'd discuss it with Zanele, but I already knew she would prefer us to live closer to the hospital.

She hated my being on the road. How often had she reminded me that she didn't like it, this hard, dirt road? How many horror stories had she recounted about the quiet roads? It was usually safe during the day, but she was always uneasy when I travelled back after a late-evening shift. She needn't be, I said; nothing was ever going to happen to me. It was at moments like these that Zanele felt obliged to make it clear to me just how white I actually was. She tried to warn me, to get me to be careful, vigilant.

Secretly, I knew she was right, but I didn't want to give in to the bogeyman. Certainly not during the day. It could weaken me, get in my way. I had to make myself useful during the day, just as I'd been taught to do at home. That he sometimes stole up on me at night was something I couldn't do anything about.

I turned the volume knob to full; I mustn't think about it. I had had an unusually pleasant day at the hospital. We'd held lengthy meetings, gone through the figures for the half-year, and discussed the most recent Aids statistics. We had meetings like the people in the nearby Dell building had meetings. Ours were about the corpses of children; theirs, about computers. All in all, only five dead children had been brought in over the last six months, and that was great news. Albert noted that they'd all come from the same region. Sadly, we already knew that the police wouldn't be looking into it any further.

I searched for Mike amongst the roughly twenty attendees. He must have forgotten the meeting, or had there been something he couldn't get away from? That was his problem: he had to, and would always, finish off his own work. Because of that, he was always working more than the approved number of hours that operations can be carried out in succession. He couldn't have cared less. I liked his stubbornness, and the way he set his own rules at work.

While I was searching, I hung around the other men, sizing them up. It gave me something to do during yet another pointless discussion about the hospital's financial problems. Subjects like this were raised at every meeting. After all, which African public hospital didn't have financial problems these days? Another regular item on the agenda was hygiene. And it was just as boring. UNICEF had even decided to offer a prize for the most hygienic hospital in Africa. As if that would motivate us.

An attractive specialist, whose name I didn't know, sat to the right of Albert. I watched him attentively as he laid his proposal on the table. He had too much hair on his head for his age. I don't know how he came up with it, but his suggestion for a burns shower chamber wasn't bad, as we had certainly had victims in the unit at least three times who had needed one. We were working with one fire blanket. The chairman made a note to look into the cost of the chamber.

The solitary traffic light on the road turned red. I looked at the closed heavens: a rare starlessness. It could be a heavy night. From behind the steering wheel I couldn't guess the height of the clouds. The clouds were overlapping; the moon didn't have a chance of getting through. I thought about the kiss on my forehead, there, imprinted in the centre, but not visible through my heavy fringe. Wouter's lips had placed it there afresh, every night. Again I felt his right hand smoothing my hair back with a brief gesture, to clear a space. I sat up straighter with my foot against the pedal.

I pulled myself together, but for whom?

The only way the moon could make its presence felt was by painting a very faint silver lining on the clouds — the clouds that garnered their power from their numbers. What is a cloud? Or two? Or ten? Only thousands together are significant. And even then, even if they rage together, even if they pour for hours on end the whole night through, nothing has changed come the dawn; no one has really heard them. But in Africa this doesn't just apply to clouds.

According to Zanele, it was due to not eating enough. Personally, I thought it was something to do with the night shifts. I was trembling all over. She suggested I take a bath. I agreed and walked upstairs. Zanele was worried about me being cold on a warm December morning like this.

I turned on the tap and started undressing. I was covered in goose bumps. I let myself sink into the hot water; it felt nicer than the air around me. My eyes were heavy from the nightshift. I had trouble keeping them open.

I was startled awake by Zanele's voice. Three times she called my name while she turned the tap off. I sat up and saw water on the bathroom floor. Shocked, my hand sprang over my mouth. She apologised. She had heard the water running, but couldn't have guessed I hadn't turned the tap off.

I looked at her, confused. She threw a couple of hand towels on the floor and said she was going to get a mop. It was only once she'd left the bathroom that it dawned on me she had seen me naked, that for the first time she had seen me really naked. Would she have noticed? Had she looked at my groin? I let my chin sink onto my chest. No, I had covered it well enough, but she had seen me naked. My nipples were hard.

When she finally returned I was standing drying myself. She'd been gone a while as she had been to fetch the bucket, which was still in her room. Could I help her clean up? Zanele shook her head and mumbled it was lucky she'd come to take a look—imagine if she hadn't been paying attention?

My eye fell on the carpet in my bedroom where there were also wet patches. They could leave ugly marks.

While Zanele stood mopping and I was dressing myself, I wondered out loud whether I was insured against water damage. She had no idea. Personally she wasn't insured, and she didn't know how it worked either.

'Costs just money?'

I tried to explain the principles behind insurance. We ran into problems before I'd even covered the concept of risk management. She tapped with her index finger against her temple. 'They're crazy, whiteys.'

Whites? Did she consider insurance a white concept?

Before I could go into it, Zanele had taken the floor. She had heard of it before and I mustn't underestimate her. Mbufu's father had once explained it. He and his brothers had had cows, she explained.

Was Mbufu's father a beef farmer?

'But with lightning, big lightning, they stood under trees.' She leant her left elbow on the mop while her right hand made a gesture across her throat, right under her chin. 'All of them,' she added.

'Jesus, were all their cows hit by lightning?'

She nodded and made the same gesture again with her right hand, across her throat.

'And? Was he insured against natural disasters?'

She tipped her head back and looked towards the heavens. That there was a bathroom ceiling in between didn't seem to faze her. Her lips made a rueful line. 'Can't.'

She was right, I thought. You can't insure yourself against the God of Africa.

Part II

In an absolute panic, Zanele ran into my bedroom. She was up before the sun, which was unusual. I must come with her, she said, over and over. I asked what was going on, but she was too agitated to answer me.

I followed her downstairs, through the kitchen, and along the path to their room. She pulled her blue beanie from her cardigan pocket for the few metres out on the path. Inside their room, Shanla was bent over the washbasin. Zanele was beside herself; she pulled her beanie off and let it fall on the ground. She didn't understand what was happening. What should she do?

'Just leave her alone,' I said. She'd probably just eaten something that didn't agree with her, or maybe she had a stomach bug. It was nothing serious.

Shanla looked relieved once she'd thrown up. I wiped her helpless little face with a wet tea-towel. She smiled. Zanele still couldn't relax, and said it must have been yesterday's dinner—maybe she hadn't cooked it enough.

'Don't worry yourself about it. It's out now.'

She shook her head. She couldn't hide her unease.

'It isn't serious, Zanele. It happened to me often as a child, too.'

But there'd been different reasons for that.

I said it would be best if Shanla just went back to bed; sleep would do her good. I walked back along the path to the kitchen. Since I was already downstairs, I put the kettle on. Zanele came in shortly after. Shanla had fallen asleep, but she was still concerned about her.

'It's nothing really, Zanele. Don't worry yourself.'

She looked at me gravely. I had never seen her like this—a weakness had surfaced in her, and weakness didn't suit her. But maybe that's what happens to all mothers when they're worried.

It was good that she had fetched me. I told her she should always come and get me if anything happened, or if she wanted to ask something. She nodded and said she always did. And she'd taught Shanla to do the same. 'Always ask what you don't understand.'

Zanele tapped her lips. 'I told her "That's why you have mouth in your head".' I nodded in agreement, and said she should stop worrying now I'd told her it was nothing serious. She shrugged her shoulders. 'Just wait, when you have own daughter.'

It dawned on me that she hadn't made the connection between the empty pedal bin and childlessness.

The same ghastly feeling as before overcame me. Maybe I should make it clear to her now, to avoid awkward situations in the future. I decided to return to the topic of what was missing from the pedal bin. She'd been curious enough about it.

'It was caused by a medicine. My mother took a drug during her pregnancy, when she was expecting me.'

Zanele nodded unconvincingly.

'It turned out to be very damaging. Hundreds of thousands of women had taken it.'

Zanele nodded again, as if all of a sudden it was becoming clearer.

'In principle, you shouldn't take any drugs when you're pregnant.'

'*Yebo*, like drink,' said Zanele.

'Exactly!'

What was the medicine for, she asked. 'Mother sick?'

'Sick? Don't be silly! *That* would have been understandable.'

I told her how my mother had had two miscarriages in between the births of Alex and myself. When she fell pregnant with me and heard of a drug that might prevent miscarriages, she had taken it.

Zanele looked vague. I was going too fast for her. I tried to find a different way to explain why my mother had taken the rubbish. To make it easier, I left out that it was about a hormone. I had no idea how to explain that. I indicated my groin. Her eyes followed my hand. 'Children were born with abnormalities to their reproductive organs. Mainly inside.'

It didn't matter that it was only six in the morning; Zanele was now wide awake and listening attentively. I took a sip of my coffee; it was still too hot. I had to hurry.

'You?' asked Zanele.

I grimaced and pressed against my abdomen with my left hand.

'No good,' I said.

Zanele stood, frozen.

I said I should hurry.

She nodded; she knew I had a busy week. I decided to take my coffee upstairs, which I almost never did.

I remembered how I'd tried to use several pads at once; the flow was so heavy that I'd been afraid of bleeding to death. I became drowsier and even more light-headed. Wouter had had me admitted.

When I came to, I was told that my womb had been removed. During the operation it had become obvious that the whole organ was a mass of inflamed tissue. I was familiar with the X-rays of inflammations like that, but this was one I didn't want to look at. It was gone. Without my even knowing it—just pulled out, cut from my body, in a matter of minutes. Wouter went into unnecessarily elaborate medical details, but I didn't want to hear about them. My left hand rested in his, and I kept my eyes shut.

Should he let my parents know, so that they could visit me? My parents at my bedside—I couldn't bear the thought of it. I wanted to scream that I didn't want that, but I didn't have the strength to produce even a normal voice.

He'd wait and see; maybe he'd let them know later. First I had to get my strength back. He's just pretending, I thought. I didn't want to go into it then. I thought about down below—I must have a nice scar, unless they had rushed the stitching. Were there blood-soaked pads between my legs? I felt nothing; the whole area was numb. One great empty space must have been created in my belly—a permanent void.

They came the next day. Luckily, Wouter stayed in the room. How cosy—colleagues, family, all at my bedside. I said nothing and didn't stir. Not when they entered, nor when my father kissed me on the cheek. He went and sat down. Uninvited. Maybe that's a right you have as a parent—to sit when you're visiting your child in hospital. To always sit, whether the patient likes it or not. This patient was pretty angry, furious even, with everyone and everything. And especially with them.

My mother remained standing; she didn't dare sit. Looking at her, I knew I had the right not to love her. She had given me good reason not to trust her.

There was only one chair; but if there had been a second, I still wouldn't have allowed her to sit. She didn't even have the right to visit me. What did she suddenly want from me after all these years?

I wanted her to leave. Leave and never come back.

Or should I thank her? Take a seat and thanks, mama. I'm miserable and have no hope of ever having children, but thanks. 'Ach, having children, it's not that great.' What would she say? That this, too, shall pass? Because everything passes. But not my longings, mama. What do we do about them? Thank you very much, and much love. To put on a postcard. But she's not getting a postcard. She's not getting anything any more. She'll never see me again. I can't do anything about the fact that she is seeing me now. It's not possible for me to stand up and say that I'm leaving. And sending her from my room would take too much strength. Just so long as she doesn't sit down, I thought.

Without my noticing, she'd moved even closer, and I

could see the corners of her eyes were teary. I felt nothing. I'd done my best for long enough. We didn't belong together; she'd made that clear to me often enough. She had her own life; I had never been much more than an interruption.

I was in pain. The numbness was wearing off. Moving hurt, as did lying still. My hair annoyed me, lying half over my eyes. I didn't have the strength to push it aside. She knew it annoyed me, but she wouldn't dare touch me. Apparently, she knew that, too. We looked at each other. My father broke the silence to ask Wouter a couple of medical details—which, to my surprise, he coolly went into. They discussed me as if I was their patient.

From my drowsy state, I suddenly heard my mother's voice. She said that oma Anna would like to come. I was startled into wakefulness and tried to speak. 'Leave me alone.'

'Now, now, Joni,' said my father. I turned my head more to the side, towards him, since he was still seated on the chair. On the only chair—where Wouter should have been sitting—there he sat, still trying to tell me how to behave. I sought his eyes and smiled at them. Drop dead, I thought.

Over the course of the day they came, one by one, but I didn't say a word—not to Andre, or Alex and Miri. Not that they'd done anything wrong, or that they'd had anything to do with it, but I'd decided not to talk any more. Once or twice I nodded or shook my head, if an answer was totally unavoidable.

Oma Anna came the next morning. She was shocked—I could see it in her face. She tried to hide her alarm. Would it be too much for me if she stayed a moment, she asked. I shook my head. She understood that silence was good for me, and didn't ask any more questions. I didn't have to make an effort; I didn't have to say anything. My arms lay next to my body; my hands rested next to my hips. Oma laid the palm of her hand on my left hand.

I wondered how she was. Whether she'd had to walk far to get here.

Coincidentally, Wouter asked my question for me. Nothing was too much trouble if it meant being with her granddaughter, she said. She loved me.

The least awful were the times when there was no one in my room. Or someone I didn't know. Then it didn't matter that I lay there like a wreck feeling miserable.

Hours later, a woman came and stood next to my bed. She said her name was Jet. In one hand was a basin of water; in the other, two cloths. She'd come to wash me. I couldn't have cared less. Apparently, my lower body was naked, so she could start straight away. She pulled something warm away. A sanitary napkin, I thought. I felt tepid water trickle between my legs. Since I couldn't sit up, I couldn't see what she was doing. I felt a cloth. She grasped my right leg and pulled it carefully to one side.

'I can reach it easier this way, dear.'

It was fine. If she looked inside the hole, she'd see one huge, hollow space. And then if she said something I'd hear the echo.

'I could preserve it.'

'What, dear?' asked Jet.

'My uterus.'

Jet looked shocked.

'Or I could put it in a box in the cupboard. Or in a jar with a lid. Maybe it would keep longer that way. And eventually you could add some water, but you wouldn't have to. The jar could still go in the cupboard. But maybe then I'd forget it, if I never saw it. So it would be better to keep it in view.'

Jet never came back. Wouter did—as a doctor. In a hideous, stand-offish tone, he spoke about my 'condition'. I allowed myself to pretend I was coping when I wasn't; I allowed myself to find a way to accept the unacceptable. But not him—he had to stand by me. I voiced my frustration, but he didn't understand what I was talking about. There was no longer any point in arguing.

I stood drying myself far too hard. Everything was different this morning. It had begun with Shanla not feeling well, and now I was showered but still hadn't brushed my teeth. The towel chafed my body, my hips, my belly, but I couldn't banish my pointless memories.

Sneezing, she walked through the house. I asked if she wanted the nose drops. She shook her head. Having a cold every year was healthy—you shouldn't try and stop it.

'But look at yourself—your eyes are watering!'

She didn't want to hear any more about it. It was a 'spring-clean' for the head; she was even glad to have it. I went back to my book.

Usually, when I sat reading she didn't interrupt; only afterwards would she ask what the book was about. But I could sense she was hanging around the living room. There was something she wanted to talk about. Her exaggerated cough wasn't caused by her cold.

I asked what was up. It was as if she'd been waiting for me to ask.

No, it was nothing.

I nodded and went on reading, but she was edging closer. The gap grew smaller: there was less than a metre between her dust brush and me.

If she really had to dust the living room right now, it would be better if I left.

Zanele shook her head. I should stay.

Tickets for the big National Lottery had gone on sale this morning, she told me. Gibsan had convinced her—it was very exciting—that she had to be in it at least once. He was going to drive to the village to buy tickets this afternoon. He was going to treat her.

I looked at her, intrigued—I wasn't sure why she was telling me all this. If she'd prefer not to be paid for, she could take some coins from the naked man's dish.

That wasn't the problem, she said. He was also buying tickets for a couple of friends. Since the queues were so long, they had set up a system: taking it in turns, every month, to buy the tickets. In the National Lottery you chose your own numbers. He had shown Zanele notes from his friends. Gibsan had said that she should also make such a list, with seven numbers, and her name on the top. Her eyes pleaded with me.

I tore the empty part of the last page from my book and walked to my bag, which had been placed under the stairs in the passage, to get a pen.

I had often seen my colleagues rushing around with the tickets. My lucky numbers, Albert would yell, and he had also told me about the enormous queues on Friday afternoons. It was badly organised; there was only one day on which you could buy tickets. He always let someone else pick them up. As far as he was concerned, the tickets could be even dearer; the entire population didn't have to take part.

I wrote her first name and surname on the piece of paper, and asked whether it mattered to her what the numbers were. She shook her head. Whilst I scribbled down seven numbers, she said she wouldn't know what to do with a million rand if she did win. I lifted my head. Would she leave?

My breathing quickened, and suddenly I felt warm. I'd begun on the numbers without thinking; now I hesitated about finishing them.

I asked if she'd heard the story about the lottery winners from around Umlazi some time ago. She looked surprised. It had been in the papers. A black family had won, and the whole neighbourhood or, rather, the whole township, knew about it. That same evening, a couple of men came demanding the ticket. The father of the family had, naturally, not co-operated. So they raped the youngest daughter. Pleading with them, on hands and knees, he'd handed his winning ticket over. Zanele was silent.

To hide the terrible thought that had sprung to mind, that maybe she wouldn't stay here and live, I said I was telling her this as a warning. 'If you do win, don't tell everyone.' She nodded, and said that the chances of her winning were very small. I pressed the paper into her hand. She threw a satisfied glance at it and held it tight. Her watery eyes smiled happily at me, and with a quick movement she pulled her apron off. She set her blue beanie on her head, with the apron clasped between her legs.

You can't kiss with a cold, I thought, as she hastened outside.

Mbufu walked along the path to the kitchen at a snail's pace. He was up early for him. I got a deep, throaty noise in response to my 'good morning'. Unshaven, as usual, he threw a quick smile in my direction — the sort of smile that I still couldn't place. I didn't know what he meant by it, let alone what he thought about me. He repeated the noise, and I nodded. It was beginning to sound like a conversation. In which case, I could ask what was he going to do.

'Nothing.'

Always the same; always nothing. If he had had work, he would have been a different young man; he wouldn't be wandering around so aimlessly.

Was something up, he wanted to know. I told him what I'd been thinking. His black eyes looked at me. I asked if there was anything we could do about it. There was nothing to be done. To my surprise, he had thought about it. It was a sickness, he claimed. The biggest illness in this country wasn't malaria or Aids, but unemployment. A thought like this from Mbufu's head? That dusty head?

I pushed my glass of apple juice across the bench. 'You might just be right about that.'

Mbufu laughed without showing his teeth. 'And that goes for the whole continent,' I added. It took just a bit too long before he nodded, giving me the impression that he didn't know the word. I asked whether he wanted anything to drink.

'If I want, I take.'

How stupid of me, indeed—offering refreshments to someone in their own kitchen. This masculine body was living in my house.

When I installed myself on the bench that evening, Zanele relayed what she had heard on the grapevine. Eco-toilets had been installed in her former township. She had plenty to say about it: it was so good for her girlfriend; it meant less illness for all the children. I had read about the government project, that finally facilities would be installed. 'How did you manage without?'

Zanele pulled a disgusted face. 'I'm not going to tell!' she said with a loud laugh. Sometimes she would burst into laughter about things that just weren't funny. She would pull a face like a teenager and laugh unashamedly. She could obviously see the humour in things that I couldn't.

Her buttocks bounced cheerfully towards the fridge. She moved as if there was music playing. When she turned around, I told her about the brief conversation I'd had with Mbufu that morning, and that I thought it should happen more often. I asked whether she was familiar with his observations on the biggest epidemic in the country. Only her eyes responded.

I relayed what her son thought about unemployment. Her expression betrayed her disbelief. And even if he had said that, she said, he hadn't thought of it by himself. I looked at Zanele, shaking my head. She wasn't being fair: she always belittled him, and she had to stop it. She had already convinced him that his head was full of dust; I'd wanted to talk to her about that for a while now.

'Didn't ask you, girlie.'

'Oh, it's like that, is it?'

She kkk-ed, but this time she wasn't getting away with it.

'You'll break his spirit.'

She threw me a disapproving glance. Just like my mother used to, I thought.

She muttered in Zulu that, actually, he didn't have much more than dust in his head. She nodded as if to confirm it for herself.

'What do you expect if you lie on road all day, on dust? You become dust. Inside and out.'

How could she talk about him like that? Her own son?

'Why belittle him like that?' I asked louder, irritated.

She didn't respond. She was, after all, a mother.

Despite the fact that I remained sitting on the bench, we didn't speak to each other again. Zanele cooked without paying me any attention. Once it was ready, she put my plate down next to me just a little too hard. I was startled. For the first time ever, she didn't say 'Eat up'. She continued to ignore me. As she left the kitchen she took her big bunch of keys from her pocket. She locked the kitchen door, shutting the outside path off from the house and from me.

At the end of the working day — I was packing my things ready to go home — I realised that I hadn't seen Shanla for at least three days. I had no idea why. I hadn't done a night shift in a week; I'd been at home on time every day. I hadn't seen her, nor even heard her, not on the path and not through the small kitchen wall that separated their room.

As I drove into our street, I greeted the sentry on the corner. His drowsiness was palpable in his slumped stance, and the slowness with which he lifted his hand in order to wave back didn't promise much, either.

At home, I threw my keys on the naked man and my bag on the floor. I walked straight through the kitchen to the little path to Zanele's room. I knocked on her door. She yelled that she was coming; dinner was already waiting. But it wasn't dinner I was interested in. I wanted to see Shanla; I wanted to know what was going on. I walked back to the kitchen. Was it something to do with our discussion about Mbufu? Was Shanla away? Away for a couple of days? Without my knowing about it, had she gone to her father, perhaps, like Mbufu sometimes did? I bit my bottom lip. Would Zanele have sent her to get money? Ill at ease, I poured a glass of apple juice, and spilt some. I took a sip from the full glass on my way to the living room.

The inner kitchen door creaked. A moment later, Zanele stood in front of me with her blue beanie on her head. To my surprise, she was also wearing her shapeless sweater. Was there going to be a storm, I asked. She let her head sink, threw a glance at her sweater to show that she understood what I was getting at, and said that she thought so. She began holding forth about the significance of insects flying around as a forewarning of a big storm, and her reasons for being well prepared, when I interrupted to ask after Shanla.

An irritated expression slid across her face. 'Pox.'

'Pox?'

'*Yebo*, Shanla pox.'

'Has she got chicken pox?'

She stared at me, dumbfounded. She obviously didn't know the word.

'Wind-pox,' she answered. Were we talking about the same thing? Was the name something to do with the infectiousness of the illness? Would the wind carry the illness from one child to another? Since I didn't respond, she tried a Zulu word.

That was it then: chicken pox. But why did she have to stay in her room?

I was given a long explanation about what someone looked like with chicken pox—as if I'd never seen it before. She wasn't worried about infection. I couldn't believe the child hadn't been allowed from her room for three days for the sake of vanity. Shanla could easily play without other children on the path. She still needed fresh air, didn't she? Zanele shook her index finger back and forth; there was to be no more discussion.

'That is insane, Zanele!'

She threw me a stern glance. 'Could I just look in for a moment, just to say hello?' I asked. She raised her index finger again. I shouldn't challenge her. Carefully, I edged my way towards the path.

'Eh?'

I ignored that as well.

A strong hand on my shoulder forced me to turn around. With some urgency, she told me that a girl with chicken pox had to hide, otherwise she would never be 'wanted'.

'Suddenly you care about what men think?'

Happily, I saw a trace of a smile on her face. 'Need them to make children.'

It could be two weeks before her skin was unblemished again. Did she have to stay in the room for two weeks?

Zanele nodded.

I had never heard of such a thing. All I remembered was that I hadn't been allowed to play with other children. And that was only for a couple of days. I had infected my mother, though. She had been about thirty; she was very ill, while I hardly noticed it. She'd even been scarred by it—one big one next to her right eye, which I could see when we sat in the car and she hadn't put on her sunglasses. That didn't often happen.

According to Zanele, it was already late—she didn't know how late—but late enough to have dinner. I agreed, and made my way back towards the living room. I went and sat at the empty dining table. I waited for my plate with my head between my hands. Zanele's feet shuffled over the floor. Suddenly, a plate with vegetables and white beans was in front of me.

Sick together. You could say it was the only thing that we'd ever shared.

'I don't want it.'

'Ehhh? You eat. Don't whinge, Joni.'

Even though I liked beans, I didn't feel like them now.

She hovered like a waiter anxious about his guest. 'You like that, Joni. Come on.' I turned my head to one side and looked her in the eyes.

We'd never done anything together, I thought again. One year going to piano lessons, and chicken pox. That's not normal, is it?

'Eat, Joni,' she said, while she slid a steel fork between my fingers.

'If you can do these yourself ...' She pointed to the pile of papers, books, and rubbish that she had made in the centre of my study. The rest of the room was neat. Unperturbed, she remained, pointing at the pile. She'd been nagging me about it for a while—that it was time to give the study a good spring clean. The time had finally come. I promised we would tidy up after dinner. In the kitchen, she passed me a glass of fruit juice. I put the glass down, grabbed the rubbish bin, and sprang on to the bench. Zanele told me that she'd been angry with Shanla today. She had used make-up.

Her index finger slid over her eyelid. 'Here,' she said, 'and on lips.'

Shanla was far too young for that. I asked where she'd got it from. Shanla's girlfriends from the street had come and put it on; they had sat playing with it in the path. Zanele had scolded the girls and said that she never wanted to see them again. Shanla was angry, but Zanele was even angrier. Not on account of the stuff. But because they had taken it from the mistress of the house where the mother of one of the girls worked. We meant to take it back, the girl had said, but Zanele wouldn't hear of it. She had asked Gibsan to take more care in the future. If he didn't leave the doors open the whole time, the children wouldn't be able to get inside so easily.

'That is nonsense, Zanele—as if he had anything to do with it. The girl can always get inside; her mother lives there!'

Zanele shook her head. 'No! No, Joni, never allowed inside. Not even in kitchen. They cook food in bedroom. Inside only for work.'

I couldn't believe my ears. They had to prepare their food

in the bedroom? How dirty. It didn't make much difference, added Zanele, because all they got was *milliemeal*—corn porridge—three times a day. Again, I didn't understand any of it; everyday things in Africa were still a mystery to me. I wouldn't go into it now; it was a strange story.

'I totally agree with you', I said, 'Shanla can't wear make-up. But just be glad that her skin is unblemished again.' I finished my juice. Zanele nodded, and I told her about my mother who never had to put anything on her lips because she naturally had such an attractive line around them. It appeared I'd told her this before. Zanele said that I also sometimes had a line around my lips. It cheered me up; it was one of the few things that I'd gladly have from my mother.

'Only evenings,' she said.

'In the evenings?'

'Yes, in blue.'

I gave her a shove. But I had to admit that, over the course of the evening, my lips often turned blue. She wondered if it was from the cold. 'Not only from that,' I answered.

'There is someone shut up in my heart, in a chamber, behind a valve. You have valves and chambers in your heart. Sometimes he doesn't want to be there any more, and then he pushes so hard on the door that a leak springs. A leaking heart-valve causes blue lips. We call it "blue breath".'

She looked at me insolently. 'Is not because you're doctor, I believe stories.'

Why didn't I make a start on the pile, she nagged. It wasn't such a bad idea; I could at least begin. I put the empty glass in the sink and walked to my study.

Most of the papers could go. I had no idea why she'd

included the Dutch–French dictionary. That can go back in the cupboard. Not that I'd use it often but, back in the cupboard. Photos taken in the snow. That was one pile. What were they doing here? Jesus, how cute. I saw how much Alex looked like papa. Especially the nose. And the light eyebrows; he had those from papa. Miri and me simultaneously giving Andre a kiss. He was standing in the middle, smiling broadly. We were in profile — Miri was a bit smaller than me, with the same fringe on her forehead.

Looking at these wasn't going to achieve anything, I knew. I turned the photo on the top of the pile over so that the shiny white under-side was facing upwards.

Even with the photo turned wrong-side up, I could still see them. Why hadn't they kept in touch? Why did they accept my absence? They had no problem living without me, with my non-existence. Maybe it had been difficult to accept in the beginning, but you can get used to anything, it seems. Even an absent sister.

Andre had tried once; he had called me. He was angry that I'd dared to leave just like that. I said that it was better for me. He asked for my number, but I told him I didn't have one yet. I already knew that I wouldn't give it to him. I didn't want to be confronted with anything any more. I looked at the pile of photos with the turned-over photo on the top. I had to decide whether to throw them away or not. I wanted to keep them.

To my left, I sorted the things that I wanted to hang on to. With my right hand, I fished a diary from out of the pile that Zanele had made. An old diary, which could go. '*Apple syrup, apple syrup, apple syrup. Friday, Saturday, Sunday.*'

No normal diary. I remembered why I had brought it with me, why I couldn't leave it behind. My monthly cycle. It seemed like a joke now. I can't imagine that my gynaecologist ever intended to do anything with it. He especially wanted mucus noted; mucus could indicate ovulation. My stomach turned. The trouble I could have been saved. They should have told me sooner. Before we started thinking about children.

Damn.

Her bare feet were encased in dark-blue shoes — with pointy toes and a low heel — which were far too small for her. She could barely walk in them. Her ankles threatened to roll over with every step. She had squeezed herself into a low-cut floral dress. She was too heavy for it. The dress was cut in two by a small belt across the middle, creating a blouson effect. Instead of her beanie, she wore a hat — a red hat that clashed with the rest of her outfit. I didn't say anything; she had done her best.

Only when she came to shut the kitchen door a couple of minutes later did I ask why she'd dressed herself so smartly. She allowed her fingers to briefly glide over the material of her skirt, and smiled.

Her niece, Tisha, had died.

'You're not going to a funeral in a floral dress?'

'*Yebo!*'

She always wore this dress to a burial, whether it was good or bad that the person had died. I looked at her. 'But it's never good?'

She nodded, full of conviction. Today was an example of 'good'. Tisha had been beaten by her husband for years. 'Drink,' she added. Now it was over — over for ever.

Was that the niece who had lost a baby because of alcohol, I asked. She nodded. 'Wasn't enough drink for baby, that's right.'

'FAS,' I said. 'That's what it's called. Foetal Alcohol Syndrome, we call it.'

A bitter laugh filled the kitchen. 'You see, we sick, and all whites do is think of name for it. That's all they do, think of names!'

So that's what we're working for, I thought. Despairingly, she stood opposite me. She fell silent.

'Did he beat her to death?' I asked calmly.

Zanele nodded, as if it was the most normal thing in the world.

She would lock the gate to the path, she said, as her fingers sought the right key amongst her bunch of keys.

'Is Shanla going with you?'

Both Shanla and Mbufu would go with her. She hoped to be back before dark.

Yesterday's leftovers would have to suffice for me; they were in the fridge. I said I'd manage. She pointed towards the kitchen cupboard; there should still be some bread. 'I'll manage,' I repeated. Maybe I'd even eat at the hospital for once — it had to happen one day. She pulled a disgusted face.

Mbufu shuffled past along the path to the gate without saying hello. His face was indifferent; he'd shaved himself for the first time in weeks. He held a shirt in his hand; I'd never seen him wear one. For some reason, when I looked at him I only saw body parts. I didn't see an arm, but a shoulder, an elbow, a hand. Maybe it was his muscularity or the rhythm of his movements.

Zanele had also noticed that he hadn't said hello. She

called him back to the kitchen in a loud voice. He returned like an animal with nothing to fear. 'Ehhh?'

'What ehhh?'

Bickering broke out between Zanele and her son. I didn't want anything to do with it. His aggression was in conflict with his easy-going nature; it didn't fit his demeanour or his body. Mbufu took some milk from the fridge. He objected to going, but Zanele said he mustn't complain. It wasn't as if he had anything better to do. He yelled something in Zulu. Zanele went and stood directly in front of him, and took the milk carton from his hands. She stuck her index finger commandingly up in the air. She also switched to Zulu. She never wanted to hear that again. If he ever dared repeat it, she'd never want to see him again. Mumbling, he left the kitchen.

The little one stood unseen, stationed outside on the path. She had heard everything. She didn't dare look up, but waited until her mother gave the signal to leave. She had put on her white blouse and a dark-red skirt. On the end of her skinny legs were neat shoes. I complimented her: she looked very pretty. With a beaming face, she asked why I wasn't going with them. She got a gentle clip on the shoulder. Had she gone crazy, said her mother. 'It's nothing to do with Joni.'

Shanla's lips trembled. I confirmed that it didn't have anything to do with me and that I had to go to work. Shanla nodded. When she got back tonight, she'd have something to show me. She lifted her heels from the ground to make herself taller, and whispered in my ear. 'In my jar.'

'Good,' I said, and hoped that, in the meantime, whatever creature she was talking about would succumb to oxygen deprivation.

Zanele turned the lock in the steel gate, and the three of them slowly walked away. I remained standing for a moment in the pathway. After a few steps I saw Zanele remove her ladies' shoes.

Mike had twice said that he liked my breasts. I hadn't responded. It only made me think of Wouter, who said once as a joke that he wouldn't have been able to choose if he'd had to. Not between my two breasts, but between my buttocks and breasts. He loved curves. I let both my hands glide over my buttocks, back and forth a couple of times. There's not much of them left, I thought, as I stood before the big garden window. I had to admit I liked the leanness; it suited who I wanted to be.

What would Wouter think of that? He'd probably be concerned, say that it wasn't healthy. This never would have happened if he was around; it was as if he had set my boundaries, that he'd known exactly what I needed. And yet I never felt that. I never had the sense of having lost control over myself or my body. It was precisely because I knew that he looked after me that I felt a certain freedom. I could surrender myself to him. His control protected me. With him around, eating poorly wouldn't be an option. Why had that changed now? Why couldn't I look after myself?

I noticed that Zanele was working without gardening gloves again. Gibsan had probably needed them. She had weeded and pruned, and she had watered the plants using a bucket as a watering-can. The door to the garden was open, and I heard her humming; it was the same tune as always.

She started when I walked into the garden. She hadn't

expected me. She said she had just been thinking about me. How I loved it when she said that.

'Not nice, about mother.'

'Oh well, that's just the way it is ...'

'I know, but not nice.'

'No, but it was never really right, Zanele. There had always been a distance between us.'

We didn't go into it any further. There wasn't much more to explain. There had never been any warmth, and I couldn't explain it properly anyway. We stood close to each other. Because she was holding twigs in her left arm, it looked as though her belly was sticking out a bit.

'What are you looking at?' she asked belligerently.

'Nothing, nothing. I'm just looking at your tummy. That's okay, isn't it?'

I said that there was always an obvious difference between tummies that had held children and those that hadn't.

'Oohoo, I was fat then—super fat!'

I asked what I had never dared to ask anyone. What did it feel like?

'Big, big!' Her lower teeth flashed in the sunlight.

I stuck my hands out in front and started waddling—as if I had a heavy belly, as if I could only straighten my back with difficulty. With my hands folded on my enormous belly, I struggled to go forwards. I curled my lips—that felt right—and walked around the garden while Zanele was in stitches. She was roaring with laughter, and I walked towards her.

Was I imitating her? Yes, I was imitating her carrying Shanla, but at the same time I wasn't. I liked walking pregnant through the garden. Zanele took my arm and waddled with me. She tapped my buttocks. 'Bum out,' she said.

'But I don't have one!' I yelled. She tapped again. 'What's that I can feel then? Eh?'

Bum out. That made it harder to stick your stomach out. Two women waddling around the garden. All at once she started imitating contractions, waters breaking. She let the twigs fall and collapsed on the ground, moaning, screaming. I was beside myself with laughter. I almost shat myself. She roared with laughter again, and said that that's exactly what it felt like—like shitting yourself. 'That's what is like, Joni!' We lay on the ground together, weak with laughter, as if it would never stop. I felt wonderful, wonderful because it was years since I'd laughed like this. And because I was with Zanele. We were laughing, even though she knew what had brought me here. I felt small; the world was no bigger than the two of us, here together in the garden.

It was hot, very hot; there was nothing I would have liked more than to take my clothes off, just like when I was young, unashamed. But that wasn't possible; it would have been strange if I lay naked in the garden, on the dry grass, with my hand between my legs, afraid of pissing. We looked at each other with aching stomach muscles. We lay close beside each other—she on her back and I on my side. I said that she was sweet.

No matter how I tried to forget our discussion about my body, it wouldn't go away. I felt awful. One way or another, it made me sick and I developed a fever.

Early in the morning, I rang the hospital to say I wouldn't

be coming in. Albert was shocked; it was the first time I'd done that in all these years. Zanele knocked uneasily on the bedroom door and hurried towards me when she saw that I was still lying in bed. I rarely used blankets here, and now I was completely wrapped in them. She sat on the edge of my bed. She said my lips were blue again; she would go and make me a cup of tea. I didn't want her to leave.

'Right,' she said, then she would get up just to open the upper window behind the curtain a little; she thought fresh air was important. I said I found it too cold, but she ignored me. She lowered the curtains again, and came and sat back on the same place on the edge of the bed. The breeze, blowing through the small upper window, made the curtains flutter a little. The bright sunlight streamed inside through a split, creating a broad white stripe across Zanele's face. I said that, for the first time, I could see what she would look like if she was white. She pushed her hand to the place where only Wouter touched me, right under my fringe, against my forehead, and she nodded as if she felt what she'd expected to find—a hot head. I was raving.

Still, all our talk had been good for something; finally, I could now see what I was. A wreck. A wreck fit for the big scrapheap in Soweto. Zanele laughed. 'That's only for cars.'

But I could just slip in between them; no one would notice. A shiver ran down my spine. I mustn't sound so desperate; she hated that. Only the vultures, with their sharp eyes, would immediately find me in their perpetual quest over Africa. They could have me.

My eyes filled. She wiped a tear away with her finger and then left her hand there, on my face. She asked if I was in any pain. I nodded. I rubbed my lower back; I always had a horrible, cold feeling there. Could I just roll over a bit, asked Zanele. In a couple of movements I turned onto my stomach.

She pushed my shirt up a little. I felt her warm hands glide over my lower back; I would never have suspected they would be so soft. A bit higher now, her right hand carefully felt my side, the spot where my right breast began. I rounded my spine so that my upper body was slightly raised. She could touch me.

The curtains fluttered back and forth. The breeze, stronger than usual, came to meet us through the upper window. The weak stream of air made me listless. I felt lighter, and my eyes shut.

Something flies in through the upper window. I can't see it, but I hear chirruping and I recognise it: it's that tiny bird with the beautiful colours, bright and light, dazzling. First he circles the room, and then he comes over next to me and hops onto my bed. I start, and tell him that he has to go, that he doesn't belong here. The bird chirrups again. He doesn't want to go. Why he wants to stay is a mystery to me, and I sit up, trying to shoo him to the window. Disagreeing loudly, he flies the other way. Only when I get really mad and start waving my hands can I get him towards the curtains that I open with a tug. It will be a struggle to get him out through the small window, so I open the door to the balcony. But he doesn't understand that he'd be better off in his own environment, in the open air—without me. When he finally flies out through the window, I wonder what in God's name he wants from me, why he wants to be with me. He sits on the edge of the balcony. When I go to shut the curtains, he seems to look at me sadly — it isn't nice of me, looking inside can't hurt. I want to lie down again. Before I turn around, I look at him one more time — and, yes, damn it, he starts dancing. Dancing in the air. To make sure he doesn't get it into his head to fly in again, I start to shut the balcony doors. He flies at them; I grab the handle and pull the door shut. Too late.

I stroke his wounded bill, his back. Why do you want to be with me? He doesn't make a sound, just stares up at me. I stroke his little head against my cheek. I shouldn't shoo you away. You fit perfectly in my right palm.

I got up in the afternoon, showered, cleaned my teeth, dressed, and walked downstairs, feeling better. It was too late for coffee which, apparently, Zanele had also thought. Whether or not I felt like tea she had already started making it. She said that I looked a bit better, and I hesitated to tell her about the bird in my room.

Shanla came and peeked around the corner looking for her mother. She was in good spirits, ran to us, and asked if she could go and get her book. When she was gone, I took another sip of my tea. Zanele said she appreciated my teaching Shanla. She asked who'd taught me everything when I was little.

I told her how, during my school years, I'd often dropped in on oma Anna to chat, and that afterwards I'd always be given music to discuss with her in detail the next time.

Didn't oma Anna live with my parents, she asked, surprised.

I understood Zanele's indignation. Taking your elderly father or mother into your home and caring for them was a sign of respect. That's if you had a roof over your head. Grandparents liked not having to do everything for themselves; at the slightest excuse, they'd call one of the many grandchildren running around and ask them to fetch a drink or pass something.

'No, we don't do that. There are special houses where the elderly go and live together when they can no longer look after themselves. But not with their children.'

She was obviously not impressed. 'Oma is strong?'

'Well, strong, for all that she isn't alive any more—she died just before I left—but she was pretty strong, yes, in spite of the things she'd been through.'

'Which things?'

'In the war. A branch of my family was murdered. Only oma Anna survived, with her husband.'

'Miracle of miracles,' as my mother put it, and on top of that oma Anna fell pregnant—miracle of miracles. But after everything he'd been through, her husband turned out to be very ill and, next thing you know, there was oma with a newborn baby—miracle of miracles—and her husband, whom it seems had been called Andre, dead.

I saw that Zanele didn't completely get what I was talking about.

'Oma black?'

I burst out laughing.

'Yes. Black. You said war and things.'

'No,' I couldn't even imagine oma Anna as black. I would have liked to have shared this with her—we would have laughed about it.

'The war wasn't about colour, Zanele. It was against the

Jews—the Jews had to be wiped out.'

'Eh?'

'Because they were different'

'You see! Like blacks!' She had grasped it immediately, but I hadn't seen the similarity straight away. She was right—it boiled down to the same thing. The history of Western Europe naturally meant nothing to her. Did she even know where the other continents were? Maybe I should fetch an atlas so I could show her where I came from. Saying I'd be back in a second, I ran to my study. She mustn't think I was leaving it at this. I returned to the living room with an atlas under my arm. In the meantime, Shanla had nestled up to her mother with her reader. She asked if we could start. 'Just a moment,' I said.

I turned the pages and opened the atlas to a double-page spread of the world map. Zanele nodded—she'd seen it once before. Shanla wanted to know what it was. I pointed to South Africa. 'We're here,' I said. Shanla looked fascinated. Zanele watched what I was doing as well, even though she had seen it before. I circled the African continent with my index finger. 'This is Africa.'

I drew my hand over the oceans, saying, 'Water, water, water …' and then slid my finger upwards and showed them where I was from. And where the war that I had been discussing with Zanele had been. 'Long way,' she said, which was true.

Shanla asked what the other things on the map were, and we ended up talking about America and then Asia—a continent where the people also looked very different. I told them about colours and eyes. I pulled the edges of my eyelids upwards at the sides—Shanla had to laugh. Zanele kept concentrating on the map. Shanla asked her mother if it was true about the eyes. Her only evidence for the existence of the Chinese was an atlas.

Not far from where people were brought in, Albert had drawn a chart on a rectangular board. To avoid upsetting patients and their family members, there were no headings above the three columns. The order of bed numbers was clear enough for us.

Patients from the last column usually ended up on the operating table or in a casket.

I enjoyed working with patients from the central column the most. Cases from the first column we often left for the interns. Against the rules, of course. With a patient from the third column, all four of us would hover over their bed. Often we'd consult a surgeon to see what could still be saved.

That's how I'd met Mike—bowed together over a half-dead patient. He set about his work assertively and with a quiet confidence that reminded me of Wouter. We fell into conversation that afternoon after the patient was transported. And, for the first time in a long while, I realised I felt like sex.

During the moonless night that followed, I found myself thinking about Mike. A night even blacker than the night's when power failures plunged everything into darkness. I should do something about it. I thought about the best approach—how best to arrange a date, without our colleagues knowing.

While I was making my plans, I heard a rustling on the roof. I tried not to pay too much attention. After all, it might just have been birds. Or the strong night wind. My thoughts wandered. I could no longer concentrate on Mike or a plan. Increasingly strange shapes of people and faces that I had seen during the day appeared before me, and the vengeful eyes of men. I seemed to be lying on my back with outstretched legs, petrified, afraid to meet the hour of reckoning. I clasped the edge of my bed, stiff with fear. Guilt—it had to be paid for. It was astonishing that I could feel guilty for something I hadn't done.

When I tried to share the details of my sleepless night with Zanele the following morning, she retorted, 'How anyone know you not Afrikaaner?'

Confirming my fears, she explained to me what would happen to the country if all the blacks took to the streets with their kitchen knives. I tried to laugh it off. That morning, with huge bags under my eyes, I drank as much coffee as possible.

Zanele was taking care of practical things. She knew that the lightning rods on the roof were often knocked down during the night. It was reasonably easy to climb onto the roof from the big gate next to the front door. Sometimes people even tried to take portions of the rod with them—God only knows what for.

The first thing Zanele did early each morning was go and stand outside, with her beanie on, at the right distance from the house, to see what the rods looked like. Once, we'd had to replace them all, and she'd arranged this straightaway with Gibsan. I'd asked her whether she was really so afraid of being hit by lightning, or was it that she just couldn't bear knowing that something wasn't where it belonged.

She didn't answer.

Shanla had seen an enormous bird in the Afrikaaners' garden, further up the street. 'As big as me,' she added, excitedly. She was walking around in bare feet again — I had to fight the urge to say something. That big seemed an exaggeration.

It was true, she yelled. I must believe her.

I insisted that it was hard to believe: African birds weren't *that* big. She held her hand up in front of her left shoulder. If there really was a giant bird walking around that came up to her shoulder, she would have to show it to me.

Shanla shook her head.

'Why not?'

She looked away. The Afrikaaners seemed friendly enough to me — we always greeted each other when we met in the street. I couldn't think of a reason why I shouldn't take a peep over the hedge into their garden. Shanla tried to wriggle away and ignore my suggestion as casually as possible.

'Why not?' I asked once more.

She stared at the kitchen tiles. 'Not with me.'

I came closer. We looked each other in the eye. 'Why not?'

My expectant air unsettled her. She began chattering. Happy and the others often made unkind comments to her mother. She'd heard them herself — sometimes when she was sitting with them, in the afternoon, under the big corner tree. They said there was something not right about it. My mouth fell open. What did they mean exactly, I asked. Just, answered Shanla, that we didn't dislike each other.

'Dislike?'

I must know what she meant, she muttered. Suddenly, I was the child that needed something explained to me; but there was, apparently, no time for that now. She hurried along the path and left me behind in the kitchen.

I walked upstairs with a strange sensation in my stomach. Zanele was in the upstairs passageway with her dust brush. Her technique seemed more to have the effect of re-arranging the dust rather than removing it. I didn't care: in the end, everything looked fine to me.

Without responding to her 'hello', I walked behind her to my room. I didn't feel like talking. Again she said 'hello'. I couldn't pretend there was nothing wrong. In an irritated voice, I asked her what in God's name her girlfriends had against me.

'Oohoo, easy, Joni.'

I hated that go-easy-ing. She should just tell me — to my face.

In her slow drawl, she explained that it was nothing personal. Certain things had developed over the years.

'Jesus, Zanele! Just tell me what it's about! Are you giving me the flick? Is this your big exit? Is that why you barely wave if I happen to drive past when you're all sitting on the corner? Is that it?'

She fell silent. I felt like saying that I was obviously too white to eat with in the evenings, but I shut my mouth. Zanele's shaking head was expressionless. I took it as confirmation, and slammed the bedroom door shut behind me. For once, I glanced in the mirror standing behind the door. I saw myself. Poor soul, oma Anna would say. I stood there for a moment.

This was my family. No, only indoors. Here we could like each other, secretly; could talk to each other like friends do. In the light of day we were acquaintances, but only on the path. And that was the one place I saw Mbufu, who didn't belong indoors—imagine the scandal that would cause! What I wouldn't give to have him here, here in my bedroom, on the ground. I'd like him here one evening. Just one night. I imagined what it would be like—what it would be like to fuck him.

Poor soul, I heard again. I shouldn't be so self-centred. It was worse for Zanele than me: at least my work was outside the house, where no one even knew her name. Whereas she had to justify herself: say that it was only for the money, that she only talked to me because I needed it. To prove it, she'd tell them everything—all the boring details. Not that it was relevant, but discussing my infertility would be a reasonably entertaining way of passing an hour under the big tree on the corner. I provided accommodation and expenses; and, yes, it was scandalous that I lived by myself in a big house while she slept with her two kids in the lean-to. But better a lean-to than no lean-to, friends. I should just forget it. I had to appreciate what was going on, and not let myself get caught up in it.

And because I knew what she was like, I knew she'd do the same.

She'd made biscuits from white corn. She asked whether I wanted to take some with me to the hospital.

'To hand around?'

She looked angrily at me from under her beanie. She thought it was about time that I started eating something during the day. She wrapped the corn biscuits in foil, and stressed that I should bring them back if I didn't like them. Shanla was crazy about them. The foil-clad parcel turned me into a school-kid again. For how many years in a row did I leave the house every day with lunch packed into my bag? But never with anything I liked.

Some children got chocolate sprinkles on their bread, but not the Jinskys. They got cheese. Cheese, cheese, and more cheese. No discussion entered into. My mother would spread a whole loaf, and leave it sitting on the kitchen bench. We took as many slices of bread from the pile as we wanted, and wrapped them in foil. Of course, the boys made the biggest parcels. I normally ate half of what I had taken. Mama never asked about it. She never asked about anything.

After school we usually went to oma Anna, and we often stayed and ate. It didn't strike me as odd at the time; we liked it there, and weren't used to anything else. It was only later that I wondered why she'd had so little time for us. How had she filled her days?

Still, she hadn't treated us so very badly; if anything, she was the one who'd suffered the most. What will she be left with? No memories. No relationships. At least, not with me. Maybe she still sees the boys regularly, talks to Miri daily. For all I know, she's changed; perhaps she's realised that things can be different. But I don't fit into her life any more. Maybe she's come to appreciate the role I played over the years — something to complain about when she's drinking coffee with her friends. You've got to have something to complain about. There has to be one child who blames you for everything; the child who makes you feel guilty, even though you've always done your best. She could arouse sympathy with it, the beauty of her face temporarily clouded by disappointment. And, if it came to that, she could always allow her inconsolable mother's heart to be seen. Or the strength it's taken for her to find comfort. We were never close, she could say. And there were other secrets as well, but Joni couldn't accept them.

She hadn't looked for me. If you look for me, I'm here to be found. She could have rung Wouter; he knew where I was working. She'd resigned herself to it. She has four children, of whom one is embittered, she'd say to friends. One is not capable of living with the facts. She'd moved to Africa. Don't ask me why. Yes, to work. More than that? No, she isn't married. At least, not that I know of. Children? No, she wouldn't have any children. You can take that from me. I am her mother, after all.

The wrinkled foil lay on the car seat beside me. I had eaten the cookies one after the other. Maybe Zanele was right, and I should breakfast on them.

Corn biscuits every day behind the steering wheel.

While Zanele was bent cleaning the floor, I noticed, for the first time, a scar on the inside of her upper arm. It was a strange colour. It looked like a small, broad cut, becoming narrower at one end. You could see that it hadn't healed properly. It was in a strange spot—I couldn't imagine that she had ever shaved herself there.

Just a knife wound, she explained, without emotion.

'That's not normal,' I said, surprised. 'How in God's name did that happen?'

'The day brother was murdered, in township. I'd tried everything. Brother is not like other men. Tried everything, Joni.'

'Why was he murdered then?'

'For nothing,' she tapped me. Often, when she wanted to tell me something, she'd first give me a tap. 'Always nothing. He slept with girlfriend of boy from western part. If he know who she belonged to, ooh, he wouldn't have done it. Some people is better not to get involved with. The boy brought six others along. I was the only one with my brother. They beating and I watching. Two talking Xhosa. Killing him took all day. No police came. Police don't dare come into township. They think they never get out. Too afraid. Better if we kill ourselves anyway, if township kills itself from the inside. Women don't leave township.'

'You did.'

'Yeah, I did. Running, running, running.'

I watched her lips in suspense.

'I was impala!'

I smiled. I thought of fleeing impalas, after they'd smelt the scent of a lion.

'With Shanla on my back.' She held three fingers up. 'She was just three! Mbufu had to run—I knew he could do it. I don't tell anyone we're going; they'd try and stop us, cursing me that I want to be white man's whore. That's what they say if woman leaves township. White man's whore. Mbufu, I said, let's see who can run longest if we run together. Who is stronger, me or you. He thought it was exciting. We ran for half hour, and walked at least six. Shanla fell asleep on my back, but Mbufu kept going. Big boy! Oohoo! I knew he was strong; was strong baby, too. Strong bones. Drank lots of milk; always drinking milk.'

'And your things?'

Zanele burst into laughter. 'If you don't have, you don't have to take with you! Ha! Yeah, white bread, a jumper for night. But no things.'

I sat listening to Zanele in amazement; I couldn't imagine tying one child on my back, taking the other by the hand, and fleeing without possessions because you simply didn't have them.

'Girlfriend had warned. She told her children they leaving on long holiday. When they heard in township, big guys quickly showed at her hut, asking what was she planning—long holiday? She going to be whitey's whore? She couldn't leave. Didn't dare. Still there. Has to stay.' Zanele let her head fall.

She had told me a while ago that she'd fled the township with the kids, but now I was hearing the details. I still couldn't see why life in the townships was so much worse than life outside. There wasn't much work outside either—no income, and people lived at the same level as inside. When I asked Zanele, she looked gravely at me. 'Was okay before, Joni, but now, no apartheid—no police. Township scary. Gangs control everything. Can't do anything without gang's say-so. No freedom.'

She came and sat at the table. Not, of course, to eat. She was glueing my loose photos in an album. I had decided not to throw them away, so Zanele wanted to have them sorted out. I thought of a shoebox; she, of an album. She'd bought one in the village. Now and then she would ask who or what something was, and I'd answer briefly. Sometimes she commented on them herself, saying that so-and-so was indeed good-looking, or that Wouter didn't have a big chin at all. I didn't want to look, even though I was sitting at the same table. I was filling in the new car-insurance forms. She thought I looked like mama. 'Thanks.'

We did look a little alike—although you couldn't find two greater opposites. No, we weren't like each other, except for the shape of our faces. But certainly not on the inside. Mama was stubborn. Disciplined. Neurotic even. She cleaned her teeth after every meal. If it wasn't possible to clean her teeth within an hour of a meal then she didn't eat. Nor drink coffee. Yeah, I'd almost forgotten that—she'd clean her teeth immediately after a cup of coffee. It was an extreme form of hygiene. Or was it something to do with her eating disorder? After cleaning her teeth she drank only water. She had a beautiful smile, but it wasn't thanks to the six-times-daily teeth cleaning. I didn't do it—just mornings and evenings. I tried to recall if she'd ever made an exception. No. Iron discipline in every respect. Once she'd decided not to talk about something, it remained undiscussed. For hours, days, weeks.

You can talk to me. Only the stubbornness; maybe I had that from her. Still, we were nothing like each other. Not one iota.

Now and then, Zanele scratched her head. I could hear it because we were sitting together so quietly at the table. It sounded different from when I did it.

I couldn't insure against theft of the car, I read. Too many were stolen, so the insurance company had simply ruled it out. I read the fine print out loud. Zanele told me about 'carjacking', which had become a sort of business run by blacks who threw people from their cars as they sat waiting at a red light. 'If you're lucky, that is; otherwise: bang, bang.' I had heard the stories, too. There were even whites who used it as an excuse to drive through red lights. Zanele laughed. 'Good one.'

I didn't let it worry me. The chance of being robbed of your life for your car seemed to me to be still quite small. But not being able to insure against it really irritated me. Zanele held a photo conspicuously in the air, as if she needed more light to see it properly. I pretended not to notice. So she turned it towards me. I still didn't look up. 'Doctor?'

I went on looking at my forms.

'Doctor?'

I didn't like her calling me that.

The third time I glanced up, annoyed. She was staring at me expectantly.

I saw myself in a white doctor's jacket that was much too big for me. My hands didn't even stick out the ends of the sleeves, and the hem reached to the ground. What a smile! I thought it was so cool and, yes, Papa had once taken a photo of me in it.

Some photos were in books, others were in folders, and there were still more in envelopes. I hadn't ever been through these. I noticed how much she enjoyed looking at my photos — that was why she'd suggested this session. The doctor's jacket! And look how happy I was. Unbelievable! She laid it down again, white side up. She spread glue in every corner.

While the scent of glue prickled my nose, I thought back to how he had rung me, how stern he'd sounded. It struck me that it was the first time since I'd moved out of their home that he'd called.

I mustn't over-react. I shouldn't blame mama. Even he couldn't have predicted that the consequences would be so great. It's like that with drugs. There were victims all over the world.

Zanele scratched her head again. It wasn't elaborate scratching; she used one finger, and scratched with it a couple of times, back and forth. Did it really sound different or was I just imagining that? I should test it sometime.

Why didn't I have any photos of oma Anna, she asked.

I looked up. I hadn't made a deliberate selection when I threw some photos in with things to bring to Africa. So I had no idea. Maybe I didn't even have a photo of oma.

So, what did she look like?

I smiled. 'I loved her voice; it was cheerful. Unlike her face — there was something sad about that, because of what she'd been through.' I didn't want Zanele thinking oma looked old before her time; that wasn't what I meant. She looked good, even when she was sick. She was a lady. 'She did have some wrinkles around her eyes; but, other than that, none. People always thought she was younger than she actually was. She even had her own teeth right up until she died! She had big eye-teeth; they stuck out a little. You could see that she had always smoked — I believe from when she was twelve. She'd learnt it from her older sisters.'

Zanele spread glue on the back of the photo.

Once again, I could hear oma Anna relating stories about all the girls in the house. Her father had called it a punishment from God. She had once told me what it had been like when the sixth girl was born. Her parents were at the hospital the whole day and they, the children, had been waiting at home, hoping for a boy—because that's what their father had wanted. Their father finally returned home in the evening, exhausted. The girls had to sit on the sofa, in order of age. Once they were all sitting in a row, legs neatly crossed, he told them that the baby had been born. With an index finger pulling on each corner, he'd forced his lips into a broad smile.

'We're all going to pretend we're happy,' he'd added.

Six girls. Only one returned.

Zanele showed me a photo with myself in it. I was fairly chubby. Let's be honest—I looked better than I did now. 'Like that, you look healthy,' she said, with a glance that spoke volumes. I told her about the scales that had arrived this week at a neighbouring department. 'I got on them straight away; I hadn't weighed myself in months. Albert had made a wager about my weight, and he wasn't far out.' I didn't dare tell Zanele that even I had been shocked—I weighed the same as when I was in the first year of high school.

Zanele thought my arms, especially, were too thin; she often said that they hung from my shoulders like sticks. Sometimes she complained about my face; I should try looking in the mirror for a change, and then I'd see the sunken cheeks. But I didn't look in the mirror. I shouldn't have weighed myself, either; but when the new scales were brought in and unpacked, and I saw that they were the nice old-fashioned type, I couldn't resist.

I told Zanele my weight. It meant nothing to her. She wouldn't know how much she herself weighed; she had never been on a set of scales.

'For what?' she asked.

You could just see that I was too thin. Maybe she was right. Still, a person should know how much they weighed. Zanele, too. I suggested that she accompany me one time to the hospital so she could weigh herself, but it didn't appeal to her. She started talking about her older sister, who had once been weighed. She had come home very proud, and had told everyone. No one had reacted; no one had been impressed. None of the seven children. Not even her mother — despite the fact that this sister had been her mother's favourite, being the eldest. According to Zanele, it was a blessing from heaven if your first child was a girl.

'She looks after the children,' she explained. The thought amazed me; I was raised with quite the opposite idea. A son — your first-born must be a son. He would care for the others should anything happen to the parents. I told this to Zanele.

'Son? No! No! Son becomes man, and men walk away! Always. Just like father. Father is man, and man walks away.'

Sternly, she looked at me. 'That's the way it is.'

Son becomes a man, and men walk away; father is man, and man walks away. She was exaggerating. It's probably what happened with her family. True, she never talked about her father; but then, I seldom talked about mine. There wasn't a lot to say. About his work, maybe, but Zanele wasn't interested in that. All that medicine, it didn't interest her. And what more was there to tell her? How he'd always thought he was holding the reins when, really, he hadn't had a say in anything? That he wasn't especially interested in us? Not that I blamed him. He was just a man with a tiring job; he would often work until the middle of the night and on weekends.

But even if he hadn't had all that work he wouldn't have been interested in us. I don't know how I arrived at that conclusion. Maybe it was the whole picture. It was to do with focus—we were never the focus of his thoughts. Science was.

My mother wasn't.

She had to keep herself occupied, which, as it turned out, she managed to do exceptionally well. He didn't have the patience to be absorbed by us—by neither her nor us. But maybe that was a consequence of his busy work. The few occasions that he did make time for us he was usually talking. It was not for nothing that we had two ears and only one mouth. When I think back on those times, I don't think of him.

Except, that is, for our annual excursion to the hospital, the day it was my turn to go with him again. You can see in the photo how exciting I thought it was. I was 'Jinsky's daughter'. That's why he wanted to take us; it was only ever about him. He was a good person, but a good person with a typical, uncommunicative post-war upbringing. It was an upbringing over-shadowed by the great sorrow, and yet it was never mentioned or touched upon. He probably couldn't help it if all he thought about was work. As the only child of a single mother, you could well be driven to achieve. One day, you'll want to be able to take care of her. So it was down to oma Anna that Papa was so self-obsessed. And, in turn, oma couldn't really help it, either. Some people just shouldn't have had children. After all the horrors they'd experienced, they couldn't cope with it. But then what was the point of surviving?

They must have had to prove something—show that they

hadn't been dragged down by it all. Yeah, look, they'd still managed to reproduce themselves. And if the children were a mess, each and every one of them, because their parents barely spoke to them? Well, that was tough, but it would pass with the generations. That must be what they thought, if you ask me.

But nobody did ask me. And I was never able to talk about it to oma. Because there were some things you just didn't talk about. My father had brought us up just as he himself had been brought up. Where's the progress in that? I would have liked to have asked her.

She would probably have said that my parent's silence about my being the daughter of a DES user was a separate issue; that it didn't have anything to do with it. I would make it clear that I hadn't even been referring to that. But they probably did have something to do with each other. I shouldn't think about it too much; it didn't solve anything, after all.

Zanele started on the last pile of photos. I asked if she could leave me out of the rest of it. She'd just have to work it out for herself.

On opening the cafeteria door, I found myself in the middle of an arithmetic exercise. 'Let's say that every patient has, on average, two visitors a day. We have fifteen hundred patients, every visitor has one sheet—do the sums,' said Albert.

'That soon adds up,' his assistant replied, without giving the total.

One sheet?

'Hey, Joni.'

I asked what in God's name were they working out.

'I had a staff meeting this morning—it appears that so much is stolen from the linen supply, millions of rand are needed to replenish it.'

I pushed my fringe, which needed trimming again, a little to one side. 'A fine state of affairs.'

He nodded. 'They don't suspect the patients but the visitors. Except management—they claim someone's behind it; that it's organised or something.'

'Interesting,' I said, while I poured myself a glass of cola. There was no time to hang around; I had slipped out briefly, driven by thirst. And, to be honest, because a girl who'd just been brought in was driving me mad by refusing to answer questions. I left the cafeteria with a 'See you.'

Back in the treatment room with the sixteen-year-old Xhosa girl, I suggested we do an Aids test. It was one of the standard tests with rape victims, despite the fact that it didn't tell us much—the victim could already be a carrier. At least it would allow us to place a red cross on the right place in the file. She didn't see the need for it; she wanted to go back home as quickly as possible. If there were enough staff available, we'd usually wash patients. I decided today to do it myself, since I couldn't see anyone else with nothing to do. As I washed her, I thought how, over the years, it had all become a bit monotonous. Nine out of ten times our ambulance returned with a similar case. Often, the victims brought in from the townships had been raped before, but never been to hospital. They only came here if they'd been beaten as well. This girl refused to speak, so I was silent, too. I carefully cleaned her cheek; the blood wouldn't clot. What had I found interesting recently? The child struck by lightning, and the two sudden re-appearances of cholera. And the youth clubbed to death. The girl said she was going home. I wanted to do the blood test first. Her glance made it clear she'd decided not to say any more. I asked her why in God's name she was in such a hurry to get home. She hesitated before answering me. After a long pause, she told me.

This child had a child.

During the evening, I told Zanele about the linen ghost that had been emptying the hospital. She laughed uproariously. She tapped my feet resting on the rubbish bin; she had to throw away the apple peel. While my legs were swinging above the bin, I said she didn't need to make fresh apple sauce for my sake; we could just pick up some jars from the supermarket. It wasn't for me, she explained. I'd get some, but it was primarily for Shanla, who was still growing.

She asked how people carrying sheets could walk out of the hospital without being noticed.

'Yes, that doesn't make sense either; we have porters, and security. That's why our CEO thinks it's organised.'

Zanele thought about it. After a short silence, she turned to me and pointed her index finger in the air. 'Visitors have nothing to do with it; they don't have beds for sheets. The man could be right — is organised.'

'And then? Somewhere there's a whole township full of stolen sheets?'

'Maybe.'

'But if there aren't any beds for the sheets, what do they do with them?'

'Money, girlie. Money.'

Woken by the birds' dawn chorus, I walked half-naked downstairs. It was a quarter past six and already terribly warm. I longed for coffee, and turned the kettle on. I heard Zanele coming along the path.

After she'd opened the kitchen door, letting the warm air stream inside, I turned toward her. Her face was furious.

'Is everything okay?'

Mbufu's nail-biting was driving her crazy. He had already started, at this time of the morning! 'Filthy.'

Could I say something to him about it?

I really didn't want to get involved. She'd have to do something about it herself. Or just leave it. He was, after all, almost an adult. Perhaps I could just have a quick word with him. I nodded at Zanele.

Did I have any idea why he did it? I shrugged. I couldn't imagine he was scared of anything. He wasn't the type. He radiated power. Since the time he'd been showering and I had accidentally interrupted him, I'd had the same fantasy over and over. I'm sitting; he's standing. I wanted to know what fed that longing, why I couldn't succeed in getting rid of that picture.

'Just filthy,' repeated Zanele. It wasn't only that his nails looked short and dirty, but she thought the biting itself was filthy. She wasn't wrong there. The way his lips pulled back when he was biting even made him look quite frightful.

She gestured for me to wait a moment, and fetched me some trousers from upstairs. I suppressed a sigh. Just let me walk up to him half-naked, with swinging breasts — give me one minute of not thinking, of following my body's impulses.

With tracksuit pants and a neat blouse on, and a warm

mug in my hands, I walked along the path to her room behind the kitchen. I knocked on the door.

Shanla opened the door. She couldn't tell me where her brother was. He'd had an argument with their mother early this morning and then he'd gone out. 'But not on street; too early for street. I think to girl; he goes to girl a lot.' Her voice was careful, as if she'd given something away.

Annoyed, I glanced sideways. Now I'd have to wait around. Which girl? What girl lived around here?

Did I want to come in?

Inside their room, I noticed again how much noise came through their wall—we could hear Zanele cleaning up in the kitchen. Shanla, with a shirt in one hand and underpants in the other, was busy neatly piling up her clothes. Zanele's bed was one huge mess. Shanla asked if I wanted to know which her favourite pants were.

'Okay then.'

She pulled two pairs of pants out from the bottom of her pile, making it collapse. They were her only pants. She held her jeans in the air with her right hand, 'These!'

While I was looking on, my eye fell on the washbasin a metre behind her; on the edge were some of my tubes of cream. I didn't understand it—I wasn't missing any. How did she get the lotions, I asked. She turned her head to the washbasin.

'From you. Mama said I can have the empty ones you throw away.'

'What do you do with them?'

'Play! Madam play!'

I swallowed. I decided to give her a full tube soon. Then

I'd also show her how and where she should rub it in. Shanla concentrated while I went on looking around their little room — at Mbufu's things, and the bed he slept on. She still held her jeans aloft, and repeated that these were the ones she liked wearing best.

'Not the cotton ones?'

'No, these are nicer.'

But they were also warmer. That's why I would have thought she'd wear the cotton ones. She had to think about that. I was startled by the creaking of the door to their room. Mbufu?

Bloody wind again. I walked towards the door. I'd come back later. Shanla looked surprised; she hadn't thought I'd leave so soon. She began busily rummaging through her things to try to keep my attention.

'I got this from you!' she called out loudly.

Curious, I turned back. At the sight of my halter-top, I thought immediately of Zanele. I could see her face before me again, concerned, as she had stood in the doorway of my study. In her left hand was my ecru-coloured halter-top; with her other hand she knocked on the door. With my eyes, I'd asked her what she wanted.

Zanele held the top up. 'Washed too hot,' she said, her voice softer than usual. I nodded; that happens. Only when it was unfolded did I realise that I couldn't even wear it as a navel-length top any more. She felt terrible, and told me that the same thing had happened once to Happy, and that she'd had to go and buy a new top.

'This is from the Netherlands, so that would be a bit difficult.'

She laughed shyly. It would never happen again, she

promised. I nodded, and asked if maybe Shanla would be able to wear it.

In the meantime, Shanla had pulled it over her head. It already looked better than when she had first been given it; she had filled out since then. While she went and stood in front of the mirror, I thought back to when I had bought it.

Wouter had suggested getting three in different colours; he liked the style. I loved shopping with him, and I needed his approval. He noticed things like the right fabric, style, and colours. We'd bought my favourite pair of jeans the same Saturday afternoon — a low-cut style that showed a tiny bit of thong when you bent over. He loved that. The flaring legs made them very elegant. Even now, when they were old and threadbare, I still loved wearing them.

At the end of a Saturday afternoon like this, collapsed on the couch in a heap of plastic shopping bags, we would congratulate ourselves on being good consumers. And if we weren't too tired, there'd be wine drunk and love made.

What was I laughing at, asked Shanla. I started.

'Sorry, what did you say?'

She made a sound just like her mother sometimes did.

Didn't I think the top suited her?

'Yes, beautifully.'

She twisted herself around so that she could see her rear view in the mirror. Just as she'd done when she'd first got it. Then she'd worn the top for a week, uninterrupted, despite her upper body being still too small for it. Her mother had to wash it every evening, and in the mornings she'd pull it on again.

'Do you still remember when you first got it?'

Shanla nodded in the mirror.

Albert rang. Thanks to the general strike, he'd been stuck in traffic for hours. It had taken me much longer than usual, too, and half the staff weren't in yet. Reassured by my arrival, he vented his exasperation at the umpteenth strike of the year. Not only the drivers of the mini-buses that served as public transport here, but the mine workers were also taking part. I wondered why we had so many strikes.

'Because they infect each other. That's the problem here.' I bit my lip and decided not to say anything.

'They wake at sunrise, they sleep at sundown. And in between?'

I ignored Albert's provocative tone.

'Joni?'

'Yes, I heard you. It's busy here, Albert.' That's the sort of chicken I am, I thought. I don't even dare to ask him to use a different tone of voice.

'And in between, not a fucking thing. Not a fucking thing, Joni!'

It was obvious he had no idea what he was talking about—no idea of just how much was fucked in this country. I ignored his comment. I asked whether I should take over his whole shift so that he could return home. Turning around was impossible; he was stuck. After we had hung up, I wondered again how the mine strike had caused such bad traffic problems. I had noticed on the way in that there were a lot more people walking around than usual. Maybe that had something to do with it. People had decided to become pedestrians instead of miners for a day—a day of daylight instead of darkness. Someone tapped my shoulder. I immediately turned around.

'Doc?' The umpteenth toothless youth.

'Fighting?'

He let his head fall in the affirmative, and with both hands in front of his mouth began his explanation. He was stupid enough to want to work today. And, what's more, to say so.

With a gesture, I indicated he should follow me. Not that I could put his teeth back in, but I did want to do something about his bleeding mouth.

While we were walking along the passage towards an empty room, I heard a din in the waiting room. Angry yelling in Zulu and Xhosa filled the department. As we walked past, people put on exaggerated coughs, just as they usually did. As if I had nothing to do, damn it.

For the first time after a day at work, I arrived home so tired that I could barely manage to get out of the car. Suddenly, Gibsan was standing there. He opened the portico. I smiled at him, and said that I was completely knocked out. Was it something to do with the strike? 'That, too,' I answered. 'Thanks to it, I've had an awfully long day.' He said that the security guy hadn't shown up because of the strike. In the meantime it was pitch black. Now he'd mentioned it, I realised I hadn't seen the guy sitting at the sentry-point on the corner.

'What difference does it make?' I muttered as I hoisted myself out of the car.

Why didn't I strike, asked Gibsan.

No one had asked me that yet. Tired as I was, I started to explain the regulations; that people in essential services aren't able to strike. Which was only right, I added, otherwise I'd have been without nurses. Gibsan nodded.

After wrestling my way through the warm air, I slowly

opened the front door. I asked whether he still needed to come in. He shook his head; they'd had an argument today. Mbufu had emptied out Shanla's cream when she'd wanted to use it. The tube of body lotion that I'd given her—Mbufu thought it stank. Of whiteness, relayed Gibsan. I shook my head. It was coarse of Mbufu—a body lotion that stank of whiteness!

The argument was about being stricter with her son. He thought Zanele should be stricter. The boy went too far, according to Gibsan. My head nodded heavily in agreement, but I couldn't be bothered going into it now. He'd have to be satisfied with this short conversation.

Inside, I threw my keys on the naked man and my bag on the ground. I walked up the stairs like an old person, in a straight line to my bedroom. I allowed myself to collapse on the bed. There I lay, for the umpteenth time, by myself in a double bed.

Maybe I should fall asleep without washing the filthy day from me; just fall asleep until the African sun woke me again. But my teeth also needed cleaning. A whole day without eating left a bad taste. I didn't have the strength to get up. What a fucked life, I thought. I stink, and am starving to death. But I'm too tired to eat. Because I work myself to death all day.

I've become a slave.

A white slave of Africa.

Her humming woke me. I could barely see her; it was much too dark. Because I didn't know how long I'd been sleeping, I asked her what the time was. 'Night,' was all she said. Stupid of me —she couldn't know what time it was at night. I asked why she was here. She pulled something from her head and started talking. Blackie had warned her. Despite the fact that they'd argued, he'd still dropped in on her. I'd come home exhausted and hadn't even eaten. He'd seen that no light went on in the kitchen, while Zanele had left dinner ready for me there.

'How sweet of you, to drop in like this.'

She was concerned, and wanted me to eat something, even if it was only a sandwich. 'The strike, it was a disaster. I had four hours' overtime.'

She kkk-ed.

A quick turn to try and get a glimpse of the clock on my bedside table sent a sharp stab of pain through my back. 'Shit!' My hand gripped it.

'Stay there, don't roll over, Joni. Is not good …'

In pain, I lay on my side and looked into her black eyes. She rubbed my lower back.

'It's nice, Zanele, nice that you're here.' I wanted to ask if she'd come and lie next to me, just for a moment.

'This bed is too big for just me,' I said softly.

Zanele began whispering also. I had to do something about that myself.

With a sigh, I let my eyes fall shut. I couldn't, not by myself. Zanele began humming again, very gently. I felt her hand against my cheek. I held mine against it and, while she softly went on humming, allowed her fingers to glide over my lips. Two fingers carefully started circling while my mouth slowly opened.

Part III

I t was only when I saw Zanele carrying the large basket on her head again that it struck me it had been raining for a couple of days in a row. 'Deep summer,' she called the period of endless rain that came after the butterfly month. The basket full of clean wet washing rested squarely on her head. She told me Blackie was giving her a lift: he had to go to the village, and he'd be able to drop her off at the drying shop. He'd even promised to pick her up afterwards. I didn't like the sound of it—Gibsan driving a friend's old bomb without a licence.

'Shall I take you—on the way to the hospital?'

'How do I get back, eh? I still have to wait for Blackie.'

She was right. I hadn't thought of that.

We'd agreed ages ago that she'd never walk back through the rain as so many women did. If it was raining I'd drop her off and pick her up. If it wasn't compatible with my shifts she'd just have to wait or take the bus. Public transport was mini-buses with a piece of paper with the destination stuck to the windscreen. The big piece of paper on the windscreen interfered with the driver's view, but placing it on the left-hand side would have been too much trouble. Zanele thought the bus was a waste of money and, as she pointed out, she would still have had to walk through the rain because the bus stopped so far from our house. At first, I'd thought we could wait together at the drying shop—until I'd tried it once.

From the outside we could see dozens of people. The drying shop was busy.

Even as I was getting out of the car I could tell from Zanele's demeanour that this wasn't a good idea. She said it would be better if I waited in the car—it was too busy inside. I insisted on going in with her so she wouldn't have to wait alone.

We stood in a queue made up entirely of black women.

It was my first time there. Zanele was uneasy. After a couple of minutes it started.

Two women near the front of the queue started calling out to me. In Zulu. Back then, I barely knew Zulu and could hardly understand them. Zanele became more uncomfortable. I asked her why we couldn't just go on talking. That afternoon was the first time I was ever conscious that she didn't want to be with me. There, right then, she didn't want to be with me. I couldn't blame her. Everyone was staring at us.

A large woman shoved my shoulder. 'Maids only!'

Loud laughter filled the drying shop.

In my broken Zulu, mixed with Afrikaans, I asked her to leave me alone. I got another shove—a big one. Zanele took me to the back. It would be better if I left. 'You don't belong here,' she whispered. It was my first summer in the country and, naïve as I was, I stayed, convinced that nothing would happen. Zanele shook her head; I tried to ignore the disapproving look. It was only when another large woman, who was already waiting in front of a dryer, started spitting in my direction that I decided to leave.

I ran through the rain to my car. She didn't want to be with me. I couldn't blame her. It's just like the washing itself, I thought: mixing whites and coloureds just didn't work. I was in the wrong place.

After sitting staring out of the windscreen for ages, I saw the two women who had been in front of us in the queue coming outside. Zanele must be almost finished. How did they get home, I wondered, how did they keep their washing dry? They pulled garbage bags out from nowhere. The baskets went into the bags. The bags were knotted shut. With their hands against the sides of the bags perched on their heads, the women walked back through the streaming rain. As straight as candles, with heavy flames on their heads, they walked along the highway.

Zanele threw her full basket onto the backseat and sat in the front. She struggled to get her seatbelt shut.

'No more mixing together, Joni.'

She sank into her seat and glared out the window.

I drove into our street as the sun was setting. I nodded at the guys sitting chatting in front of the driveway to the corner house. The last remaining rays of daylight in the heavens had vanished by the time I'd parked. Inside, I threw my bag on the ground. The naked man trembled as my keys hit the tray.

She wasn't in the kitchen. It was already six-thirty.

'Zanele?'

Shanla was the only one to answer. In bare feet, she came and said that her mother had just popped out. It was the first time this had happened—coming home in the evening and finding only Shanla. Was everything okay?

'Yeah, mama's getting gloves for tomorrow.'

It had stopped raining for the moment, and she didn't want to waste any time setting to work in the garden. But what a strange time—usually she picked the gloves up in the morning.

They're having sex, I thought.

I went outside and sat on the path with Shanla. It was hot; the way it was always hot, even after sunset. From the path, we would be able to see Zanele the minute she returned. Shanla had grabbed a couple of corn cookies and a banana, and she asked if I wanted any. I did feel like something. They're having sex, I thought again.

I asked Shanla why she didn't wear any shoes when she was outside. She looked at me confidently. '*Kaalvoet* are nicer.'

She didn't know any better; her mother walked around like that as well. But it still worried me; after all, it was Zanele herself who had told me about one of her cousins being bitten. 'You know it can be very dangerous? That there are scary insects walking around that can bite you?'

She rolled her eyes briefly at the ground, which meant: 'Of course I know.'

'Your mother told me herself once about a cousin who was bitten. Did you know that?' She nodded and pulled the same face again.

'There aren't any scorpions here—they live at the Cape.'

130

It sounded plausible. Still, I wasn't sure she was right. 'I've seen the little black scorpions here,' I said, trying to get a reaction.

'Maybe, but not poisonous ones. Mama says poisonous ones don't come here.'

'Hmm. But between sunset and midnight they wander around.'

It didn't seem to worry her. I let it go, but I couldn't stop thinking about Zanele's story of the cousin who had lived at the Cape and died of a scorpion sting. With huge gestures, Zanele had related how red and swollen her cousin's foot had become. She could remember it perfectly. It looked as if red flames were coming from it, she'd said. She'd also described sweat attacks and cold fevers. I said that he would certainly have survived in a hospital, which Zanele doubted. According to her, I obviously had no idea how swiftly the poison worked. I remembered her asking if I'd ever had anyone come in at work with a scorpion sting, and I had to admit I hadn't. And still hadn't. Even when, I realised, half the population walked around in bare feet. Maybe it was true, after all, that the poisonous ones were only found at the Cape. But why would they restrict themselves to one area?

At five to eight, Zanele's feet came running. I'd never seen her run before.

There were only a couple of metres between each house, so whether you ran or walked didn't make any difference. I tried to read her face to see what was going on. We didn't interrupt her, and she ran on to her room. Shanla placed the banana peel on her lap, and broke the banana in two. She gave me half.

Zanele appeared after a couple of minutes. She excused herself for being late, and quickly started cooking. Would I come in and sit with her? The cutting board and two knives lay waiting; she threw the apron over her head. I sat on the bench and watched her body while she stood in front of the fridge.

I could well imagine that Gibsan desired her—that men in general might want her. Her movements radiated power. Her face was soft and attractive. I couldn't see her face now. I could only see her from behind—the view that men love.

My feet found their usual resting-spot on the rubbish bin. I didn't dare to ask. She turned with green, pear-shaped vegetables and some carrots in her hand. When I saw the vegetables I raised my eyebrows, satisfied. I loved them. I still didn't know the Afrikaans name for this cross between a pumpkin and a carrot in the shape of a big pear. The Zulu name Zanele gave them was long and complicated—I could never remember it.

As if the point of her visit to Gibsan had been the future of her children, she told me that she'd asked him what he thought about Shanla maybe going to school. My mouth fell open. Why didn't she discuss that with me? Gibsan didn't think it was a bad idea. Because she was slicing the carrots, she couldn't see how surprised I was.

'And you don't discuss this with me?'

She looked up. 'Of course—I am now, aren't I?'

I couldn't bear to think about Shanla leaving, and I knew that Zanele would send her to a black school far from here. We'd never discussed it, but she'd once implied that it would have been better if Mbufu had gone to school. She knew, by word of mouth, of a good school in the north — Pretoria. Just thinking about it made me see red.

'It would be good for her,' I said.

'Maybe. But she'd have to stay with strangers — I have to think.'

I hoped she'd abandon the whole idea; that she'd never find people who would take Shanla in, and that she'd never say the word 'school' again. I thought about boarding schools, and children who could only go home once a month because they lived too far away.

I was suddenly in a foul mood. I wanted to sit there without talking any more. If it did happen, of course I'd just have to learn to live with it. With this thought, I heard Wouter's voice again. I'd been shaken from unconsciousness, abruptly shaken from all my dreams of motherhood and stitched up, and what was it he'd said? That we'd have to learn to live with it. To accept it. I couldn't bear it when he said 'accept' in such a cool and controlled manner. I hated it. I was furious, and told him it would be better if he forgot me, forgot what we'd had, and forgot he'd wanted to crown our happiness with a child. He could always go back, back to his family, and they could forget, too. It would be nice to have papa at home again — without having to share him. How wonderful; almost like it used to be. Forget about the last couple of years, his wife would say to herself, lying next to him in bed in preference to being alone. She could keep him.

Zanele's cooking looked like taking forever. When she finally offered me a laden plate, I said I wasn't hungry.

'Oh? No-no-no, you eat now. Just eat. Don't eat all day, now just eat.'

I didn't want to. Zanele's school proposal had made me nauseous, not to mention the memory of Wouter's comments.

She gave me a shove that made it clear I should get off the bench. Carrying my plate, she led me to the dining room. She put the plate on the place mat. The cutlery was already there. I saw a full wine-glass and a napkin. She asked whether I felt like a cola. Pressing a fork into my hand, she walked back to the kitchen to fetch a normal glass. I was a child, a small child who had to be taken care of.

I set the fork back down next to the plate. When Zanele returned, she said I should start eating, otherwise it would get cold. I couldn't have cared less, and took a couple of sips of wine. It didn't help at all.

Zanele rubbed my back. 'Sweet carrots, girlie. Made sweet for you.'

She wanted to go to the children — they still had to eat. It was already very late.

'You shouldn't have stayed so long with Blackie.'

'Kkkk,' she said, walking away, half dancing.

Only after I'd heard the door from the kitchen to the path close did I take a bite from the tepid meal.

If she ever asked me why I'd left him, I'd have to have a good answer. It would have been easier if I hadn't loved him any more. I could explain to her that he suddenly found me charged, bitter. He shouldn't have said that we'd learn to live with it. I wanted to go on feeling the pain in my belly. And in my head. Maybe I could tell Zanele that he didn't think I was strict enough with myself; that I should be tougher. He wanted to help me with it, but I didn't want to be tough. I let myself go on longing. Longing for the impossible. How could I explain that to her? The evening I'd realised this, I decided it would be better for me to resolve it by myself, to go on alone. I arranged to leave as soon as possible.

Hurriedly, I divided my things into two: things I needed to take and things that could be thrown away. He went on talking. He would help me through this. I didn't want to go *through* anything. I wanted him to shut up. Yes, it was lousy; here he was in a new apartment, he'd left his family for me, and I was dumping him just like that. But it wasn't 'just like that', I corrected him. He didn't want to understand. He told me he loved me dreadfully and it didn't matter to him; everything that had happened didn't change anything for him. That was just the problem—nothing had changed for him.

And it didn't matter to him. How could I live with someone who didn't care that I was infertile, or that I'd been deceived since birth by my own parents? I didn't want anything to do with people who said that they loved me. Keeping the truth hidden from me for twenty-three years. I could do without this soap opera. There wasn't even a part in it left for me. It was as if he was rejecting my just-tendered resignation. He kept touching me. 'Stay away from me!'

Why was I suddenly so distant, physically? I wanted him to leave me alone—leave my body alone. He'd be better off finding a new applicant for this vacant position. Turn on the charm again at the hospital or in the faculty, I suggested.

'There are plenty of young girls around. Beautiful, fertile. You can try something new. When you always eat meat, a bit of fish is sometimes nice.'

Would I stop saying such stupid things, he asked. Ridiculous! But there was no stopping me, and I said it wouldn't be so difficult for him; he was a good-looking guy, there were enough girls who'd fall for his stern good looks. He must see that this nice apartment was better than any student hovel; that in itself would be a drawcard.

Could I calm down for a moment? 'Sweetheart', he added.

He started on about my new job. It wouldn't suit me; patients would be coming in with problems that I didn't even know existed. I looked at him scornfully. He really didn't need to explain that to me.

He glanced around and kicked the cupboard. I was alarmed; I wasn't expecting him to get angry *now*. 'I've told you how you should fill the void; I can even give you names, names of students who were green with envy because I was sleeping with you.' He ignored me. Don't push me, he said.

But I knew him; he wouldn't allow himself to be pushed now. 'It would be good if you were contactable, there, in Africa,' he said, to demonstrate that he had himself back under control. 'You must be contactable,' he repeated, laying it on extra thick.

' "Contactable" is what you have to be if you have children at school. Fuck off with your "always contactable".'

He was refusing to accept that I was calling it a day, that I was no longer playing. I was no longer a daughter simply because I should be a daughter, and I was no longer playing the girlfriend. The girlfriend who had first been a lover; that's what had been written in the script. But the script also said they would have a child. Bad script. Revise. Rewrite. Cut out the girlfriend. Replace. I gathered my CDs. He tried to stop me.

'What have you been trying to teach me? That I have to live with it? Acceptance? Then just let me go. I don't understand what more you want from me. Here, have a copy of my degree. Nice for later. That's when Joni graduated. You can show it to your son—that's important. He should think of getting one himself one day—you can do so much with it. Save lives, or ruin them—either way, that's not our problem. That's the victim's problem, and she sits on the other side of the table. Usually. But not this time. This time she's here. Piss off. Go back to your wife—get laid the way you used to. Go back; be the happy family man, play 'weekends' on the weekend and 'the week' during the week. Stop screaming? I'm talking to you! This *is* the last straw!

He followed me from room to room while I collected my things. It was driving me nuts and slowing me down—I had a plane to catch, after all.

It was inconceivable that I'd always wanted him around me; now I couldn't stand him. I remembered the time oma Anna had explained a parabola to me—the way it rose to a peak before descending again. She'd said it was true of far more than mathematics. She was right. In my mind, I put a black dot on the curved line closest to where we were now.

He walked towards the kitchen, and stood in the doorway. 'I want to get a drink of water,' I said. Piss off, Wouter!'

He wouldn't stand for it any longer. The tone I was using to speak to him was unacceptable. I asked whether I was going to be punished—was he going to take me hard from behind?

He slapped my face, hard.

The harshness in his eyes frightened me—I was afraid that I'd give in. He grabbed my cheeks. He brought his face closer, chin set, lips taut, and told me to behave myself.

I slunk away to the hall closet where my jackets hung. I could feel my bottom lip trembling as I opened the door. It had been so good.

Only one of my two jackets would fit in my suitcase. I left one behind.

I dropped in on Mike. Not that I needed anything from the surgery department. He looked uneasy when I entered. We hadn't spoken to each other for a while. Seen, but not spoken. He asked after a patient I hadn't treated for ages. I wasn't carrying any files, so he knew I hadn't come to discuss patients. I was wearing my white doctor's jacket. I asked him if he felt like coming over for dinner. Silently, he agreed. Would tonight be okay? Again, he nodded. He didn't seem enthusiastic enough to me. Maybe it was too long since we'd seen each other. I decided to see if his body still responded to me.

I left his room fifteen minutes later with a bad taste in my mouth. In the hallway I got the urge to throw up, and was only just able to suppress it. While waiting for the lift I remembered the super-sized chewing gum that I used to buy at the fair. He was so big, or my mouth so small, that there was nowhere for it to go. I knew that swallowing was my only option, but it was also the least attractive. I walked into the lift and could still feel both his hands pressing against the back of my head with a force I wasn't used to from him.

He told me he'd be able to find the address, but I'd still wanted to explain the best way to get there—that after the sandy roads there would be a small section of paved road, and then on the long road there would be four houses, of which mine was the last one.

Back in our department, a youth came up to me with a bloodied face and a couple of teeth in his hand. The white jacket meant I knew everything. These youths and their loose teeth drove me nuts. After a bit of a fight, there was always someone who'd lost his teeth in the struggle. 'We're not bloody dentists!'

I told him he'd have to wait.

What for, he asked. I didn't know. Not for me, in any case.

In the ladies' I swilled out my mouth and tidied my fringe in the mirror, before going to Albert and asking what we were to do with the toothless casualties. Albert looked annoyed. 'Another one?'

I nodded. He decided to make a note of it so that, for once, it could be discussed seriously. He stressed that he didn't really expect there was anything we could do about them. The youths would have to go through the rest of their lives with only half their teeth. No matter how horrible it looked, for the moment there was no affordable solution.

My pager went off. I recognised Mike's number and immediately turned the sound off. I couldn't think of what else he'd have to say. Albert asked what it was. I shrugged my shoulders. He suggested I return the call from his office.

I'd forgotten to take the yellow super-ball that I'd wanted for my maid's daughter, said Mike. Should he bring it with him this evening?

'Oh, how silly of me. Yes, please do,' I answered.

Albert was curious and wanted to know what was going on. I told him that Mike was giving me some sort of toy for my maid's daughter. He looked at me, surprised.

'Don't be too good to them,' he said. I was a foreigner. I didn't know any better, but if you were too good to them you'd ruin them.

Yes, that's the way it is—as an Afrikaaner he'd seen it so often. Well intentioned, he said, but it never ended well. This is how you make them lazy, and they become spoiled.

'I'm giving her a super-ball, Albert …'

He'd wanted to say something about it before, and now, coincidentally, it had come up. He'd noticed from comments I'd made that I had a good relationship with my maid. He wanted to stress the necessity of keeping a distance; it was very important. 'They're not used to anything else; you mustn't confuse them. You're white; it doesn't matter that you're not from here.'

I swallowed, and thought it best to act as if I hadn't heard. For his own good, I decided not to respond. I turned away. He said I should at least think about it. I answered that I was going to Treatment Room six. A man had been waiting there for an hour with large shards of glass in his leg—an accident installing a window-pane. I let Albert's door slam shut behind me. The phrase 'You mustn't spoil them' rang through my head. Cockroaches. He hadn't quite dared say it.

He'd made one thing clear: I'd have to exchange my confidence in him for suspicion.

On the way home, I called Zanele. I never said my name

when I called. Once, long ago, when I'd phoned my mother she had asked me with whom was she speaking. Zanele always recognised my voice, no matter how bad the connection. I told her that we'd be having a guest that evening. She shrieked into the phone. She could be so horribly enthusiastic. If I wanted, I could have guests regularly. I wouldn't think of it. Even having Mike come over I found too close for comfort. But, fine, I'd already laid more of myself bare. It was as if it had to happen once. I couldn't just walk into his office and ask when we were going to fuck again, could I?

Zanele asked me to let her know earlier the next time Mike was coming; she could prepare a nicer meal. The connection was lost. I rang back to say it only had to taste good, just as it did every evening. I left out the fact that it wasn't about the food.

Shanla laid the table and Zanele bustled about. I had to laugh. She asked whether she should stay—to serve, to catch a glimpse of him. It seemed unnecessary to me. What did he look like then, she asked.

'Lots of hair, big eyes, taut body. Not my type, actually.'

I hoped he'd be able to find our house—I hadn't given him any additional directions.

'Don't worry,' said Zanele. After all, you could only drive into the street from one end, and there was a guard at the door of the first house on the corner. He would show him the way, she was sure of it.

'Him! He's always asleep!'

That was true, but then you just had to wake him up.

I laughed, and asked what was the point of having a guard who was always asleep. I read in her face that she was going to defend him. She told me that lots of youths who had a normal day job had to work as guards the whole night through, from sunset onwards. She stressed that their mothers weren't like Mbufu's—the boys worked very hard. 'Can't go on forever,' she said sympathetically. The whole system of security guards was a mystery to her. More and more whites were taking on a security guard. Had I noticed that? I nodded.

She tapped her temple with her index finger. 'It's balmy! Blacks risk lives for whites?'

I pinched an olive from a small bowl. I hadn't even known we had them in the house.

I got a rap on the fingers. 'Don't touch—for Mike.'

My eyes wouldn't close. Over and over they read the time on the small, glowing alarm-clock on the bedside table. Automatically I counted how many hours I still had. It was driving me nuts. All I wanted to do was sleep, but my mother was stopping me. Just as the thought of her had so often hindered me. I thought about her remoteness: how she'd always given me the feeling that she wasn't really there. How I'd hated it when I came out of school bursting to tell her something, but knowing beforehand that she wouldn't give a damn. I turned onto my side for the umpteenth time. My other side, so that at least for a moment my eyes couldn't look at the clock. She'd been self-absorbed, wrapped-up in herself. Children just got in the way. Like her husband did. It was just as well he hadn't had time for her. Only the hospital interested him. With them as an example, it would have been surprising if I had believed in parenthood at all.

But I had believed in it. That I could do better. Or at least differently. I'd show my children what it was like to get along with each other, that parents chose to be together, that they lived together because they liked it.

I kicked the blanket off. It was far too warm for blankets. I pulled the sheet over my shoulder and peeked at the clock yet again. Back to the hospital soon. I'd become just as boring as my father. In three-and-a-half hours I'd be going back to the hospital from where I'd just returned. That damned hospital, where black people surrender themselves be stitched up or sent away by whites. For want of anything better. Because they can't do it themselves. Because they've never had the chance. At last, there are sanitary eco-toilets in the townships, and blacks do get the opportunity to study. But they don't want to study, after all. One day, they'll realise; one day they'll realise that first they need to get rid of the whites. And they'll discover just how easy that can be. All they have to do is slam our heads against the wall, splattering our blood all over the place—our white flesh's red blood. They'll clear us up and take back their land. Clear the whites and their filthy dogs from the country, into the ocean—with their yellow corn and their brown bread.

Shanla was clinging awkwardly to her mother, so they took a long time coming down the path. Why was Shanla awake so early I asked, as they walked into the kitchen together. Zanele told me that the little one had slept badly. So I wasn't the only one.

'What's wrong?'

Shanla didn't want to talk about it. She wasn't talking at all. She'd had a bad dream, said her mother. A former friend of Mbufu's had been picked up for murder. He would probably get life. Shanla had overheard her mother and brother discussing it. It had really frightened her—not the murder, but the idea of being in prison for life. She had asked about it, but Zanele had tried not to dwell on it, instead telling Shanla she should try to sleep. She had dreamed that Mbufu was sentenced to life. She and her mother went twice a week to visit. 'So far so good', said Zanele.

But, in the dream, Zanele hadn't wanted Mbufu robbed of his life at such a young age, so she had decided to serve his sentence herself, allowing him to go back out onto the streets. I saw Shanla tighten her grip on her mother's hand.

I stroked Shanla's cheek and looked at Zanele. 'You should be proud of her.'

Shanla clasped her mother as tightly as I could remember clasping my own. Instantly, I felt the tension in my hand again. I told Zanele I had to get a move on—I was already late. The old, familiar tension stayed with me as I went upstairs. In large groups, especially, the hand mustn't be let go of. Mama allowed it, but she didn't like it. She could never have imagined that this same child would ever let go quite like this.

She should have been straight with me—not treated me like a fool.

Once again, she was showing no interest in me, which made it clear that, again, she was putting herself first. She didn't want to lose any more face; she had her pride. I'd behaved scandalously. I'd just have to sort it out myself.

But I am still your child? That doesn't change, does it? Why haven't you tried just one more time?

If she'd called, I wouldn't have hung up. Secretly, I'd have been pleased. I'd have listened as she told me her side of things. If, finally, she'd tell me her side.

It wasn't about blame—I understood that. I'd simply wanted to sit down with her. It was about the silence. Once I'd discovered what was going on, she should have talked to me.

Or sat down with me, so she could comfort me. Or I her. So I could tell her that it was okay, that I've learnt to live with it. That I wasn't angry any more. But then I'd be guilty of doing the same as she had. That's not okay—I would have to be straight with her.

She hadn't meant it; she'd never wanted to hurt me. Can I believe her, after everything that's happened? Can I believe she'd never wanted anything more for me than to have a good life? I nod and feel sad. It's so long since she's been to see me, since she's spoken to me. I throw my arms around her. My mama. Why was she so proud, I want to ask. Why had she stayed so proud for so long? She doesn't know, either. I smile, cautiously. She asks why I don't adopt a child, and I say I'm alone. A single woman can't care for a child, unless it's her fate. She nods understandingly and tells me about Miri, who has a son. Just like me; my first was a boy, she says. And my stomach is filled with jealousy, but I suppress it and ask what his name is. Aron, she says. I smile and think about a son—how often I'd longed for one. The only thing I want is a child, the only thing I think of, I want to say to her. But instead I ask how Miri is and who she is living with, and Mama strokes my cheek gently. I long for it so much, mama. My sadness is sometimes so great, greater than myself. Or is the impossible making me small?

We don't have to talk about it if you don't want to; she understands it's not doing me any good, that it's difficult for me. She knows me and, this time, expresses it.

She asks about Wouter. Why had I broken it off? I can't explain. She asks why I don't go back to him. We talk, we look at each other, and it is honest. No secrets, no confusion. It's just like being with Zanele: she is close and I can be myself.

I am not angry and I don't want to run away.

True, I'm sad. But she's allowed to see that.

Albert asked whether I knew of anyone who'd be suitable as a gardener, just before we handed over shifts. It was almost six in the morning. I immediately thought of Gibsan and his dirty gardening gloves.

Albert's gardener, who'd been working for him nearly seven years, had had an accident while mowing at a friend's. Yeah, Albert thought it was dreadful, too — there was nothing he disliked more than an unkempt garden. Apparently, there was work being done on the roof at the same time; it must have been a misplaced stone — he didn't know the details. His mouth stretched to form the rueful line that people here pulled at this sort of story. The line that meant: 'There's nothing to be done'. *Ach*, he'd find another gardener. There were millions in this country; they just didn't know it yet. But he didn't want to take on just anyone, so he was asking whether I knew of someone. I said I would check with Gibsan, although I had no intention of doing so.

He filled his mug and asked how the night had been. I had to admit that, as a doctor, he was professional and competent.

He was even friendly towards patients. I handed over three files; it had been a quiet night. He scribbled our team number on the top of the folders. I'd forgotten to do it. That was to his credit—that he didn't draw my attention to it, but just filled it in. He set his coffee cup down and started leafing attentively through the files. What was it that made him seem so unpleasant? I said good day and left the canteen. We wouldn't see each other until tomorrow—there were two shifts between now and then.

Gibsan and Zanele were sitting on the path with their backs against the wall, both in exactly the same way—legs stretched out, ankles crossed. I couldn't quite see, but I got the impression they were leaning against each other. They smiled and waved exaggeratedly.

They were doing that more and more: sitting together for a moment on the path at the start of the day, usually on the mornings that Gibsan hadn't slept in our street but in his own township, further away. These mornings he had a long journey behind him before even starting work, so he came and drank a bowl of warm corn porridge. The steel gate was left shut so that people would know they wanted to be alone for a while. If Happy or anyone else thought of dropping by so early in the day, it was clear that they'd be interrupting. Zanele's washing was hanging on the line to dry. She preferred to hang her smalls outside. Gibsan had strung a cord up a couple of years ago in the perfect spot. It wasn't in anyone's way. I only noticed it today because I stood gazing longer than usual down the path. I waved back and walked to the wooden front door. Once inside, I felt how heavy my eyelids were. It was time to take a long shower.

While I was drying myself I heard Zanele and Shanla talking in the upstairs passage. It sounded as if they were cleaning; there was definitely the sound of scrubbing, and I gathered that Shanla had to pass something. Was the little one really helping? I quickly dressed and walked into the hall with wet hair. Shanla was holding the bucket full of soapy water and walking alongside her mother, who had decided to give the floor a good once-over. Zanele was wiping invisible spots away with a cloth made from a torn shirt. 'Zanele?'

She turned and looked at me, irritated—I mustn't interrupt her without a good reason. I said that I wasn't happy about the little one carrying the heavy bucket. Her irritation grew. It was none of my business. There was nothing wrong with it. She herself had always worked—'helping out' couldn't hurt.

It wasn't a good idea to pursue it in front of Shanla.

You'd have to be pretty sharp to convince me that having a blood nose every day was normal just because everyone around you had a blood nose every day. He took my tissue. If he hadn't been such a big muscular miner I'd have given him a shove to show him that his story didn't make sense. It wasn't the blood nose that had brought him here, though—he was looking for work. Eleven years in the mines had broken him, and he wanted something different. He didn't have any training, but here at Emergency there was nothing to stop you walking in and giving it a shot. He was very muscular—yes, I had noticed—so maybe he could carry patients, he suggested. That appealed to him. 'Where to?' I asked.

He smiled, with the tissue pressed against his nose. That was for me to tell him. From the ambulance to inside, or from

148

here to the rooms? 'We have beds' I said, still fascinated by the blood nose, 'on wheels.' Okay. Out of nowhere, while we were talking, the bleeding started again. Who suffered from blood noses in his township, I asked. In good black English, he explained which township he lived in, and how everyone there — men, women, and children — had a blood nose daily.

So, it wasn't just his mates from down the mines. The township was only a stone's throw from the gold mine. There had to be a connection: it looked as if noxious dusts were being produced that caused regular blood noses, even in women and children in the nearby township. I said that it wasn't normal — that, on average, people had a blood nose once a year. He frowned. He radiated something that made it clear he wasn't impressed by a white chick in a doctor's jacket.

'Doc,' he said, his eyes challenging me. If I let him work here and his blood noses stopped, I'd be proven right.

I laughed at what at first seemed like a good suggestion, and I couldn't resist giving him a quick tap. His nose, in the meantime, was clean, so he threw the tissue away.

There was nothing more to show. 'Sir,' I said — he had told me his name but it was too complicated to remember — 'the goldmine might be damaging the veins in your nose, probably by inhalation, and after a while it won't matter any more where you work or live; you'll still suffer the effects.'

He nodded jeeringly a couple of times and repeated my words in an artificial voice. I couldn't help laughing. I liked this guy. Sadly, we didn't need anyone — not in the ambulance, not at home. Albert was looking for a gardener, but I wouldn't wish that on anyone. I said I'd have a think about it. He didn't move; he obviously thought now was the appropriate time to think. The prospect of a full waiting-room made me nervous. He would have to leave, but could he at least for the moment go and wait on a chair? He nodded, and promised not to go away until we'd discussed it at length. The gold miner had been too smart for me, and had made his problem ours. I'd brought it on myself. Not, as Albert would accuse me, because of post-apartheid ideals. But simply because I'd felt attracted to him.

Zanele slowly filled the wash drum.

Why had she let Shanla help, I asked.

'With floor?'

I nodded.

Nothing wrong with that, she said. She'd often done it herself when she was young. She concentrated on the washing. When money is scarce, children must work. 'Helping out', as she preferred to call it. She had stood on the lookout for years, keeping an eye out for police with the other children while their mothers were brewing beer in the backyards of their homes. Zanele beamed when she told me how they went about the brewing. She seemed to have fond memories of it. But I mustn't think that being on lookout didn't involve much.

She set the washing on the ground and walked to the door. She sank to the ground. She sat in the kitchen doorway, supported on her right leg. Her body had assumed a ball-boy's stance. I slid from the bench and came closer. She acted as if she was concentrating very hard on everything that happened. With her head on one side, she looked into the connecting path. As if I didn't understand what being on watch meant, she started explaining how all the children had to remain silent. Every car that entered the street was a threat. If they had even the slightest doubt, they'd yell to their mothers in the backyard. Zanele leapt up, just as ball boys do, but slower; the mothers in the yard could clear away the entire brewery unbelievably quickly, in a matter of seconds. Now that she thought about it, she was still impressed.

'Real quick,' she repeated.

Did the police ever come, I asked. She nodded. Usually, the women knew how to arrange it so there was nothing to see. Still, she remembered there was one time the police had made problems. Zanele pulled a serious face. Even though there was nothing to see, the women still had to pay, in their own way. She lowered her eyelids.

She threw the last of the washing lying on the ground into the drum. I pressed my hands on the bench so that I could easily spring back up.

If only I'd once stood on the lookout. I placed the rubbish bin a bit closer. If only she'd once involved me in what she was up to. In everything she did that she shouldn't. I stretched my legs. We might at least have known each other better then. My feet hung on the bin. She kept everything hidden. Secretive and sly. I lifted my right leg and let my foot fall back hard on the bin.

Hey!' yelled Zanele.

I'd even shocked myself.

When I held my breath, I could hear it even better. It sounded very close. As if they were sitting under my bed, or a bit to the right, over by the window. I didn't want to know what the rustling might mean. Should I turn the lamp on or not?

I inhaled deeply one more time. Rats? No, there was nothing for them here upstairs. If I shut my eyes, I could hear it even clearer. I sat motionless on the bed. Exhale? I hated this. The noises. The thoughts.

Zanele had to laugh every time. Noises of the land, she called them. The remnants of the big bang that accompanied creation. 'Water; boom, boom,' she said, while her head jolted back and forth, 'and then dry.' She stuck her index finger in the air. 'Not only for second day; still now.'

She often referred to the Zulu creation story. I didn't want to disappoint her, so I never told her we had the same story. When the wind tugged at my windows at night I knew she was right; some noises are unique to Africa. Like the howling night wind and the pouring rain. But not this rustling.

I turned the light on. Immediately, it was silent. Nothing to see. I turned the light off. A moment later it started again. There was something about it, like the scratching of a fingernail against a wooden table. But there was no wooden table. And no nail. After turning the light on and off at least seven times, I sprinted downstairs to hurry along the path to Zanele. The only thing I could grab to put on was tracksuit pants and something for my feet. Bats? They didn't have any bones, and could get under doors. They lived at night because they didn't like daylight. It was the creatures of the night giving me heart failure yet again.

I had to unlock the kitchen door, but in my panic couldn't find the key. Finally, I rushed along the pitch-black path. I stumbled, lost my balance, and almost fell over. That was close. How was that possible? There couldn't be anything lying on the path. Zanele always left it tidy. Whatever I'd stumbled on moved but didn't vanish. This was no animal. I automatically stopped breathing. It was a foot—a human foot.

Someone was sitting on the ground against the wall. I forced myself to look to the side. I'd just have to go through with it. My last seconds. I saw the whites of eyes and nothing more. The body didn't move, let alone speak. My trembling felt like the final convulsions before the end. But whoever it was didn't seem to be out to frighten me.

Who was it?

If Gibsan had been sitting there waiting for Zanele—and why not, who knew what they got up to in the middle of the night?—he'd have said something to me. No, it wasn't Gibsan. Exhaling was out of the question. I was getting dizzy. Suddenly, I heard the same rustling that I'd heard in my room. Now I realised that it came from a person. If only it *had* been an animal, a small animal in my room. I had to go back, find a way back, without remembering this, I'd forget it. We'd both forget it, this silent night-person and me.

There was no time for forgetting. The whites of the eyes stood up and came closer. A hand grabbed mine. Scream really loud, I thought. But I didn't scream. Cry! Cry really hard! But that didn't work, either.

'What the hell, you here in middle night?'

I knew the voice that belonged to the whites of the eyes—even the body. I could breathe again.

I should be asking him that, I said, with a tremble in my voice, as if all the fear in my life had collected itself here on the path and been voiced in that one question.

He made the rustling noise again.

'What *is* that, damn it?'

'Cigarettes.'

Relieved, I let my head fall back. The rustling of cigarette papers. The window above the path was my bedroom window; the noise came from here.

Did I want one, he asked, as he went back to sitting in his spot.

I shook my head.

Would I sit down beside him for a moment?

Before I'd thought about it, my body had already slid to the ground. With my buttocks on the ground and my back against the wall, my legs made the same angle as his. Now I'd be the one accidentally tripping people up. Especially anyone running. Just so long as he didn't ask me what I'd been planning, I thought. A bat in my room … what an idiot! He'd think I was a dumb bitch. A dumb white bitch.

I asked what he was going to do with all the rolled-up cigarettes. Was he going to smoke them?

It was obvious I didn't understand anything, he replied. His head might well be full of dust, but this was now his trade. His own business.

Could he trust me? Would it stay between us?

I nodded. 'Night-people don't recall anything by daylight.'

He turned his head toward me. We were almost touching each other.

'You know,' I said, 'the night-people, the people who are made of dust during the day.'

He laughed, flashing his teeth.

For weeks, she'd persisted in trying to find out how dinner had gone, and every time she asked I said that she had cooked marvellously. That annoyed her. She wanted to know what was going on between us.

'He wants to date more often, but I don't want to.'

Mike didn't know me, and I wanted to keep it that way. He hadn't even seen my scar. Thanks to my careful shaving, my pubic hair had come in handy the past few years. Still, I had to have a story ready, in case it ever came up. A caesarian scar looked similar, but that wasn't a good explanation. What I remembered of the evening was that once again he hadn't wanted to use anything, and again he'd asked me if that was a problem. Was I on the pill? I couldn't be bothered with the whole thing, and nodded. With a couple of thrusts, he'd filled me up.

I had to ask him to stay the night to get what I'd really been longing for.

Just past midnight his head sank between my legs. He pushed them wide apart. I tried to push back so that I could clamp his face between them. I lay partly on my side; I wanted to see him kneeling, his buttocks sticking out. I was sopping wet from the mixture of saliva and moisture. His right hand reached for my breast; I hoped it wouldn't be too quick.

Why didn't I want to see Mike more often, asked Zanele.

'I want to be alone, you know that.' I started upstairs to take a warm bath. I'd been cold all day, even though it was warm in the hospital and outside — hot even.

From the foot of the staircase, Zanele nodded.

My teeth chattered. She watched me, concerned. Just as long as I don't get sick, I thought. I said I'd be back down for dinner.

Zanele placed her index finger under her right eye.

'I'm watching you.'

I felt like lying in the bath for hours. I soaped my arms and felt my heavy breasts.

I had no use for them. They were round and soft, but I had no use for them. I felt my nipples. My hands sank to my stomach. There was still so much space.

I closed my eyes, and was standing again at the edge of the bath. Mama lay in it. I looked into the water. What were the strange stripes on her tummy, I asked.

'That's what you all did,' she answered.

I didn't have the elongated stripes, and my wide horizontal scar was much lower. Look, Mama, this is what you did. My right hand glided over my pubic mound, covered with hair. Since the scar, I only shaved a small area.

I opened my eyes. It was my body lying under the water's surface.

Around midnight, Zanele took the padlock from the big steel gate. She told me about going to meet Gibsan.

It had been one of those evenings when it was too late for Gibsan to return to the township. He would sleep at the Afrikaaner neighbours. She walked to their house in bare feet, and tapped on the side door of Happy's room, from which a door led to Gibsan's bed. The Afrikaaner's dog was the first to awaken. She stiffened as it let her know. She was petrified of the beast—of all dogs. Luckily, they kept him in their own yard.

After persistent knocking, Happy finally opened the door with a sleepy head. She threw an irritated glance at Zanele—as if she knocked on the door every night while they all slept. She couldn't care less. Saying nothing, Happy walked back into the room half asleep, and woke Gibsan. Hastily, he came to the door in his underpants. With one hand, he indicated he needed a second — he'd be back soon. He left the door ajar; Happy was already back in her bed. He returned in clean jeans, his torso bare, a beanie on his head, and keys in his hand. Was Shanla there, he'd asked. Zanele nodded. They'd have to be as quiet as they could. Mbufu was away for the night, she said, relieved.

She didn't feel safe as long as the dog was still barking. Gibsan whispered his theory about dogs into her ear again. They didn't belong in Africa — whites had brought the dog here — so it was only to be expected that the dogs barked and the blacks were scared. It distracted her and made her laugh. But she laughed soundlessly; Shanla must go on sleeping until sunrise. Then there would be no trace of Gibsan to be seen.

While Zanele was relating this to me, I noticed how tired she was and how much she didn't tell. I'd only just returned from a night shift, but I still felt fine. I wanted to stay awake for a while; now it was still tolerable. I asked whether he'd woken on time. She nodded, happily. I gave her a tap on the arm and thought of them having sex while the child lay there asleep. But what else could they do?

I walked out the kitchen door to the path where Shanla was already playing with Happy's daughter. They looked odd — there was something strange in their hair. It was only as I drew closer that I saw that it was pencils. They'd stuck pencils through their curls.

'Hey, Shanla, the colour pencils are for drawing!'

Insolently, she looked at me.

'We're doing pencil test!' The girls fell about laughing.

'The pencil test?'

Shanla bent over so that her head hung down, and vigorously shook her head. The pencils stayed in. She straightened up again. The girls couldn't stop laughing. I left them to it.

Zanele was carefully dusting the naked man. She asked whether she should get some cookies for me, for breakfast.

'Thanks. I'll do it myself. What's the pencil test, Zanele?'

She looked at me wide-eyed. She asked if I wouldn't first put away my keys; I'd left them lying on the kitchen bench. I put them neatly into the ugly dish. Slowly, she told how during apartheid the population was divided into groups. 'For housing and other rights.' She paused a moment.

'White was easy.'

But distinguishing black from coloured was not always so straightforward. Some coloureds were almost black, and there were many blacks who claimed to be coloureds. Now she mentioned it, I remembered that coloureds had other rights at the time.

'That's why the pencil test.'

She related how all the township inhabitants had had to stand in a long line. In turn, a white would stick a pencil into your kinky hair. 'We had to bend over, right over, like this,' Zanele bent over, just as Shanla had done outside.

'If it stayed, you were black. If it fell, you were coloured.'

'Jesus, how primitive!'

She raised her brows.

Was there a system behind it, I wondered. Did he roll them and sell them on fixed nights? I had to find out. The only person I could ask was Mbufu himself, but the only way to manage to see him again was by trial and error.

I'd still never seen him sitting on the path there when I returned from a night shift. Most likely he took to his heels as soon as my headlights fell on our house. I didn't know why I'd wanted so badly to sit with him since that first night. Maybe it was to do with the darkness — in the dark I was no longer his mother's Madam; I was just a girl on a path. Whenever I was startled awake I hoped it was by his rustlings. Because of this, the night stillness began to become a friend.

It was almost two weeks before the chance arose again. I heard him rolling papers, and leapt up with a beating heart and nervously paced up and down. What should I do? Just go downstairs? I could be looking for something to eat. No — he'd been hearing for years that I didn't eat. Even thirst was a poor excuse; I had a bottle of water upstairs. I shook my fringe from my eyes and tried to see him from my bedroom window, but it was too dark: the path was one big black hole. Even the sand-coloured pavers that I overlooked were black now. I made a noise to get him to look up.

Disappointed, I sank back onto my bed a couple of minutes later. I want him, I thought. Fast. And hard.

It was another five weeks before I finally succeeded in catching his attention during his nocturnal cigarette-rolling. It seemed that he sat there at the end of the week— maybe he sold them on weekends. I'd parked neatly after my night shift and, despite the full moon, couldn't see him. But I knew he was there somewhere. He usually returned after about five minutes. So I came back—having left a file behind in the car on purpose. I didn't have a key for the steel gate, so I had to walk right around anyway. After getting the file from the car and watching him return to the spot on the path, I acted surprised to see him. He said good day. I asked whether he still had work to do.

'*Yebo.*' Was I tired from work, he asked.

'Not too bad,' I answered, at the same time thinking that his interest was promising.

Two minutes later, we were sitting together on the path. Did he want something to drink? He started laughing; I'd made that mistake before. He lived here, too; if he wanted something to drink he'd get it himself. I apologised, and thought back to the time he'd been showering. Just the image alone made me warm.

Should we share a cigarette, he asked.

I never smoked. I didn't like it.

'Mmmm. Thanks.'

He gave me the cigarette he'd rolled, and we smoked without talking. At first it made me nervous, but after a while it felt natural. The path was filled with our silence.

More than five minutes passed, and I decided to ask him about his business.

He drew heavily on the cigarette and answered me without turning his face in my direction. It was doing well, but today he felt pretty 'shit'. He was going to be a father again, even though it wasn't something he wanted.

I stopped breathing. My mouth fell open, but nothing came out. A child? Again? How many did he have then? And with whom? Or was he bragging?

He stared straight ahead, not seeing my shocked expression. It was easy to ignore in the darkness. I wondered whether Zanele knew about this.

He sat beside me, slowly smoking, conscious of every pull on his cigarette. Nothing followed his announcement; it was obviously my turn to say something. I swallowed—maybe that would help.

After a couple of swallows, I asked him how many children he already had. He leant his head back against the wall. With his chin in the air and his gaze on the sky, he started talking.

He didn't know exactly—some 'bitches' would have falsely accused him. But there must be at least a couple. He didn't want to know them. If the girls started going on about it, he wouldn't have anything more to do with them.

'Jesus, Mbufu.'

The prick could thrust and pump like no one else. And he was fast. Faster than the speed of light.

'Why don't you want anything more to do with them?'

For the first time since we had been sitting there the whites of his eyes came closer. He only wanted to fuck—his head made three thrusting movements, accompanied by a hearty snorting noise—and the rest, he added, was their problem. Why didn't he use a condom? He laughed. It wouldn't be any fun then, would it? I should have reminded him of the endless queue of fatally ill people we saw at the hospital, but instead I started to smile. It made me think of Wouter, who had also hated them. He'd said it was like making a child wear gloves to play with play-dough. Mbufu pushed his sturdy shoulder in a seemingly friendly fashion against mine, and said that this relationship wouldn't have ended well anyway.

I agreed. It should be a law of nature. Nothing ends well. He lit another one. As I looked in the flame, I suggested that it bothered him more than he was letting on—after all, he had brought it up out of the blue. With his cigarette clamped between his lips, he said that this one actually was a really nice girl. But now she'd gone and spoiled it, too.

Another good reason to do it tonight, I thought.

I wouldn't spoil anything.

Births were usually taken care of in the townships. Why this girl came to the hospital was a mystery to me. Maybe she was in the neighbourhood, or she was scared. Two girls the same age—I guessed about eighteen—had accompanied her. One way or another, Africa always made it seem as if men had nothing to do with children. Maybe they were her sisters. Or friends. I'd find out when they filled in their details. But first a child had to be born. In all the years I'd been there, I'd never directed a birth; time and time again I'd succeeded in handing the task over to others. Plus it didn't happen that often. Albert had once explained it to me: 'They don't want any white hands involved.' The derision in his eyes made me doubt his version, but Zanele confirmed it when I asked her that evening. Birth was a holy occurrence that they preferred to keep 'clean'.

'Jesus, how insane. As if our presence was contagious!'

Zanele had nodded.

My washed white hands were now delving into the labia of a gorgeous eighteen-year-old. The drops of sweat on her forehead gave her a beautiful sheen. She was thin—skin on bone—but her belly looked magnificent. She spoke Tswana, and none of our employees could make head nor tail of it, but it was clear that a baby had to be gotten out. As I focussed on her vagina, it occurred to me that, once it had been stretched like this, it would never be small again. Would you always be able to tell that she'd given birth? That is, aside from any tears and scars?

Albert's assistant called me away. Thank God. She knew by now that I hated births. Two nurses would take over so that I could accompany her to a new patient. As I walked through the fluorescent lit hallway, I thought about Mbufu and how he, too, left girls like this—pregnant and alone. Would Zanele know?

She wouldn't be shocked. How often had she said that men always walk away?

As old as Methuselah—she was ninety-eight, she told me in Zulu when I asked—she stood before me, her back hunched. Wrinkles lined her face, but she was still good-humoured. Albert's assistant told me that this lady had walked in alone; for the rest, she left it to me. Her walking stick, which she leant on with her full weight, trembled so much that it, too, appeared to have Parkinson's. I asked her what the problem was.

She hadn't been able to straighten up for a couple of days. She quivered towards me, bringing her head closer so that she could speak more softly. I must see that she was old, very old, but she had always been healthy. She did tremble, but that was because she'd worked so hard. Sixty years. Washerwoman. She made quivering circular hand movements and said something about a tub. For sixty years she had stood and worked hard, with different white families — 'As white as you,' she said in Afrikaans. She'd suddenly switched languages, as if she'd only needed the Zulu in order to get going. Or she'd suddenly realised I was white. I found her story fascinating, but a baby was being born and there were still plenty of people waiting, so I asked her if she could get to the point. The point was, she was stuck; she had never been so stooped, she explained.

A deep sigh escaped me. This was typical of the sort of case that should be seen by a GP, not an emergency department. But they never had a GP — they didn't even know what a GP was. It was high time the system changed. Except there was no system. I shuffled down the hallway with an almost hundred-year-old Parkinson's patient on my right arm. Next, everything had to go through the wringer. She repeated the Afrikaans word to be sure I understood. And then she hung everything on the washing line. She made two pinching movements with her thumb and wisdom finger. Huge washing lines, because they were large families. And everything was just thrown into the wash — as if it made no difference. Did I have any idea how heavy the men's cotton trousers were when they were wet? It sometimes took two days to dry them in the sun.

'To the right here,' I said, to indicate the entrance to the examination room where I'd have a quick look at her back. Not that there was anything to see — but I couldn't just let her go. And then the ironing, she said. She had stood ironing for eight or nine hours in a row. Her quivering hand made an ironing movement, slowly — slower than she would actually have done it. She grabbed my white jacket by the collar and smoothed it: 'Not neat'.

She mustn't start insulting Zanele; that was all I needed. Professional defamation, I thought, and didn't respond. Would she take a seat, I asked. That was the problem: she couldn't sit on a chair any more. Fine, then just stand.

She turned side on and smiled, content. It didn't hurt, she said. But it was very inconvenient. She couldn't do anything any more. As far as I was concerned, she could count herself lucky to be so lucid at her age. Did she want anything to drink? Serene eyes watched me. She would like a sip of water. How come I spoke such bad Afrikaans, she asked. That was a bit rich! Next thing I, too , was setting aside the formalities. I was from another country, I told her. She looked at me, surprised. I didn't have Afrikaans parents? I shook my head. 'I don't have any parents.'

Her heavy wrinkles registered shock.

I grabbed a plastic cup and walked to the tap.

'You an orphan long time?'

I stood with my back to her. I hadn't used that word. I filled the cup half way, in deference to her trembling.

'Yes,' I answered. 'A very long time.'

In the silence that followed, I wondered how on earth we'd ended up on this personal note. I decided to put an end to it and to focus on her back complaint.

There was nothing to be done for her back, and if there had been I wouldn't have done it. It made a difference that she wasn't in any pain — she would never have been able to afford painkillers. There was no money for medicine, let alone for most operations. Eighty per cent of operations performed were on gunshot wounds. Cases like this — certainly with a patient this age—were dismissed outright. Over the years, I'd learnt that it was a waste of energy to pursue them. After a brief examination of her spine, I used her age and whatever other excuses I could think of to deliver the bad news.

'Tsss,' slipped from her lips.

As I advised her to keep her back warm, her ninety-eight-year-old eyes gazed reproachfully at me. What could I do about it? It was the same with the budget—it was upstairs who decided what we could and couldn't treat, whom we should and shouldn't keep alive. Family members always looked at me as if I was personally responsible, with the same expression as this practically centenarian washerwoman. The looks were more devastating than words. I hated them.

She walked back into the hallway, mumbling that the hospital was as ugly on the inside as on the outside. If not uglier. From the outside it was disgusting—dirty and poorly maintained. The exhausts from the nearby freeway from Gauteng to the north—the road that I never used—had left their black traces on the once-white external walls. Well, her 'Tsss' hadn't offended me, if that had been her intention. She obviously belonged to a generation that didn't dare to curse a white person. At least not out loud.

At the end of a day that looked like being the hottest I'd ever experienced—a thought that occurred to me daily—I returned home to find Gibsan crouched under the stairs. My eyes fell on the split between his buttocks rising up above his pants; for some obscure reason, his torso was again bare. If I hadn't known that he and Zanele already had something going, I'd think he was doing it to try to attract her attention.

166

It couldn't have had anything to do with the heat, or he wouldn't have been wearing the beanie on his head. He welcomed me to my own house without turning. I asked what he was doing. The lowest stair tread was loose and Zanele had asked if he could screw it down. I wished him luck as I went on my way to the kitchen. I was thirsty again—it had been such a hot day—and hastily pressed a bottle of water to my lips. With my head tipped back, I didn't see Zanele come in to the kitchen from the path. 'Nooooo! Joni!'

I put the bottle down quickly and took a glass from the cupboard. She started talking to Gibsan in a mixture of black languages. Had he seen Mbufu, she asked. He hadn't come home yesterday and she hadn't heard him today, either. With my ears pricked I went on drinking, agonisingly slowly. If I drank any faster, I wouldn't be able to hear what they said. Gibsan concentrated on his screwdriver, and claimed to know nothing. He asked her to move aside so that he could get closer. As usual, they started bickering. Why should she step aside, and why was he acting so irritated? He was busy, he yelled. He would kill to be able to work, just once, without being interrupted.

Slowly, my stomach filled with what felt like jealousy. Mbufu must have stayed with a girl. Had he stood, pumping her full, just as I'd imagined he would do to me?

It was his attitude that gripped me—he acted as if he didn't give a damn about anyone or anything. His sparkling eyes could look at me so deeply and, simultaneously, so angrily—and even more often not look at me at all, apparently ignoring me, which only made my longing greater. To him, I was obviously just a silly white girl who didn't interest him at all. That I provided home and income for his family didn't make any difference to him. I wanted Mbufu, but Mbufu didn't like white girls. At least, that's what he said.

The way he had looked at me on the dark path, and leant his shoulder against me a couple of times, had made me wonder. Once he'd even made me blush, which he'd certainly not seen in the dark. He'd said that I didn't laugh often enough during the day, so he rarely saw my beautiful teeth. I hadn't reacted. He'd said that he liked looking at girl's smiles.

Would we ever be able to do something together during the day? Go for a walk? Or don't the night-people have any rights during the daytime?

The same picture danced before my eyes. Me sitting and him standing. And again he was fast.

Work at the hospital had kept me busy for the last week. The departure of a number of doctors hadn't helped. Physicians as well as surgeons—including Mike—had left, exchanging our hospital for a white one on the Cape. If they hadn't gone to the Cape, I'd have thought it was the brain drain that Albert was so afraid of, with everyone fleeing overseas.

I'd had little time for Shanla—we hadn't read or played. And I hadn't spoken to Mbufu in almost two weeks. I'd nodded to him as I was driving past, but we hadn't seen or stumbled upon each other at night.

Evening had fallen, and I really shouldn't have been interrupting Zanele in her room. She opened the door with a surprised expression. Was everything all right?

I nodded. 'I could hear you were still up, maybe I could …'

Zanele opened the door wide, just as it occurred to me

that I'd come at an awkward time.

'Don't worry about it,' I said. 'I'll listen from the kitchen.'

'Don't whinge!'

I went and sat on the ground, next to Shanla. 'You never let me sit on the ground!'

She was right, but there weren't any chairs.

Zanele picked the rhythm up again as if there hadn't been an interruption. She counted off and signalled to Shanla to continue dancing. I hadn't ever seen them do this. I only knew the sounds that accompanied it. Mbufu wasn't there—he'd gone back out on the street straight after dinner. He was only there for meals. Zanele nodded at me to sing along. I'd come to know a couple of their songs over time, but I didn't dare join in.

After a couple of minutes, she stopped. She asked whether I understood what the song was about.

'About a man, but I didn't get exactly what.'

She laughed. Cautiously.

'About invisible man ...' she groped with her fingers in the darkness, and her hands fluttered. 'No one has seen him.'

I nodded.

'A type of Mike,' she said, laughing.

'Ach, shut up. You saw him walking in here?'

'Not me ... Shanla.'

Shanla turned her face away momentarily.

'Anyhow—we won't be seeing him again. He's left. For the Cape.'

Zanele looked at me, surprised. 'So is over?'

I nodded.

She struck her drum with a powerful clap. I jumped out

of my skin. She tapped four times, and then held her hand up over her mouth while she made a noise and moved her hand back and forth. I recognised the sound. Shanla started to count. Zanele shoved the drum to her. She stood up. Shanla repeated the rhythm set by her mother as Zanele's bare feet began to shuffle across the floor. She circled with her eyes closed. She sang without words. When she opened her eyes again, she danced towards me, and her hands gestured that I should stand up. Shanla went on drumming.

I stood in one movement. I let myself move. I danced.

I wanted to close my eyes. Zanele's hands circled my waist.

It was almost four in the morning—the night light was burning as usual in the guard's box at the corner house. I drove further up the street, into our driveway. There was no point looking for Mbufu—it was a Tuesday night. I locked the car and walked into the house. I immediately felt a draught. Where was that coming from at this time of night? Was it the kitchen door? Had Zanele left it open by mistake?

I threw my keys into the grey dish, and carefully walked into the kitchen. Both the interior and exterior kitchen doors were open. Strange. I looked along the path. Left. Right. Nothing. The wind must have blown them open. I locked both doors the way we usually did at night. In the hall, I threw my workbag on the ground. Tired, I went upstairs.

As soon as I walked into my bedroom, I knew. Even in the dim light I could see that everything was in disarray—clothes thrown from drawers, mattresses overturned. I had to see what had happened, and switched on the light. They must have slept through it; even Mbufu couldn't have heard anything. Or wasn't he at home?

Luckily, I'd been on night shift — otherwise I'd have been in these men's way. And they didn't like that.

There was nothing to take here. Yeah, a television; but surely they wouldn't carry such a heavy old thing out of the house? I thought I'd go and look — downstairs, in the living room. For some reason, I felt sure they'd left. I didn't know what made me so sure. Annoyed that they'd been here at all, I went back downstairs. There was nothing to be afraid of, I convinced myself; the damage had been done.

I decided to wake Zanele to show her what had happened. They hadn't even turned on the downstairs light — it was pitch black. How could they steal things in the dark? Or had they turned the light off afterwards?

The television was still there — I could see its outline in the dark. I walked through to my study; they'd probably left that in a mess, too. I froze. Was that someone breathing? Or had I imagined it?

Yes, I could hear someone breathing, very faintly. I didn't move. Suddenly, unexpectedly, I was scared to death. My intuition had misled me; there *was* someone close by, in my study.

Should I turn on the light, or freeze, or wait until I was grabbed by the throat? I didn't know; my legs were trembling and I wished I'd never been so stupid as to just walk into the house. The open kitchen door; why hadn't I realised? Any moron could see it had nothing to do with the wind — that murderers armed with kitchen knives were roaming the house ready to cut my white throat.

My left hand pressed the light switch. I had to know what had happened.

I fell to my knees and crouched beside her. She lay on her stomach. Her nightdress was shoved up to her waist. Her legs were limp, spread, as if they were spent. Her knickers were on her left foot. Her eyes were shut. She'd heard them — she'd interrupted them. I grasped her torso, and carefully rolled her over. Her head fell backwards. I looked at her face, her breasts. She was still breathing, very faintly.

I pulled the hem of her nightdress down over her breasts, and dragged her up. God, she was heavy now.

Albert was on shift, and I wasn't allowed to be involved. Her eyes were still closed; her head rested on one side. My lower lip trembled. I wanted to be there to decide for myself what treatment she needed, to estimate her chances myself. Albert's assistant left the curtains open a tiny bit — as I'd asked her to. I watched through the glass.

She was in pain. She'd shut down, and become unconscious so as not to feel anything. I wanted to hold her hands, to say that it would be okay, that I'd make sure of it — it was my job, my work. I'd be there every day, do successive shifts, stay there day and night.

I'll pull you through this, wake you up, now, or soon, but it will happen, I'm confident. I felt dizzy. I'm falling, but soon I'll wake you up, and we'll go home together. It was just a bad dream, a nightmare they've given us. You're right about men, all men; we should close off our property, make it secure, so that we don't have to be scared any more. We'll go back, to the children, to the butterflies in our garden.

One of our department nurses, Phumelele, was bent over me. Her smile was broader than usual. It was too busy for them to be looking after me as well, she said. Would I mind not fainting again? 'Doctor,' she added. It took a second for me to understand what had happened. I tried to smile, to sit up.

'How is she?'

She relayed what Albert had said. My stomach turned. I got up and rushed to Zanele's room. Finally, I was allowed in.

I stood next to her. I didn't dare touch her.

There was no point talking to her. I coughed. She didn't react. Not even with her eyelids.

The rear would be the worst. Luckily, she was lying on her back. A white sheet was pulled up over her shoulders—the white sheets I'd told her about.

Albert couldn't say exactly what had made her unconscious. He hadn't found any signs of heavy violence on her skull, although there had been a blow to the head—he could see that on her right temple.

Maybe it had all been too much for her? Maybe she hadn't been able to take it any more? There'd been four men, Albert guessed, from the condition of her anus. We were familiar with this injury at the hospital, and from it we could estimate numbers. Blood-test results were still to come. It would only take one with Aids to make this tragedy even worse than it was. Usually it was deliberate—to spread it. I knew I should still try to talk to her. I'd often told families to do this, without knowing how difficult it was. Maybe tomorrow, I thought. I always tell them there is a chance—a very small one, but a real one. After that, I would explain that we call this situation 'locked-in', that they needed to talk while there was a chance they might be heard. I shut my eyes and wanted to pray. But I didn't know how.

On the third night, I slept in her hospital room. It was unusual, but they couldn't do anything to me. I'd spoken to her that day for the first time. I'd moved closer, so that maybe she could smell me. I'd told her how I'd been searching for her blue beanie. I'd looked everywhere. On the path and in the house. Even in her room. Where on earth did she keep the thing? Shanla didn't know. She didn't understand any of it. Where her mama was, and what had happened. I hadn't told her everything.

I was afraid that Zanele's head was cold. Maybe I could buy a new beanie for her? But I didn't know where to get one. And I didn't want to stay away for too long. I'd ask Gibsan. Maybe he'd lend her his.

Albert came to tell me that there'd been a significant turn for the worse. He sounded friendlier than normal — or gentler. Maybe that was it. He let me look at her file, and put one arm around my shoulders. I liked that — the arm. The Afrikaans' arm. I nodded in agreement; it didn't look good. We discussed her condition, and neither of us could understand why she was so badly affected. Was it an incidental complication? Something we couldn't resolve?

Albert said what I was thinking. At this rate, she didn't have much longer. I looked at him. Try to distance yourself, he advised, meaning well.

Mbufu didn't want to know about it. Shanla didn't understand what I was telling her, but she was keen to come to the hospital with me. I hadn't spoken to Gibsan again; hadn't seen him myself. I had asked Mbufu to bring him up to date; maybe he hadn't even done that.

Shanla asked if I'd go with her to her room, so we could choose something nice together. I told her that it wasn't necessary: her mama couldn't see anything now. But it didn't matter; she wanted to be nicely dressed. She pulled on the only skirt that still fitted her—she'd filled out and grown taller. Her good shoes also looked a little tight. 'If we have time, we'll buy some new ones. Okay?'

Shanla nodded.

She sat next to me in the car. It was nothing like I had imagined it would be. We didn't chatter. There was complete silence. It reminded me of the times I'd been in the car with my mother—but at least then the radio had been on. She'd worn sunglasses, just as I did now. Why was there such an unpleasant atmosphere, just like back then?

Shanla was confused, unsettled. Her mama was away; she'd never slept even one night without her, and suddenly she was gone. I'd already tried to calm her by telling her that she didn't have to worry, but she wouldn't listen. Mbufu would be looking after her in the meantime, for as long as that lasted. Suddenly, it seemed, I no longer had the role I'd assumed would be mine. I'd made that mistake before. I asked her if she'd caught anything with her jar this week; she hadn't shown me anything. From the corner of my eye, I could see her cautious smile. She hadn't felt like it, she said. She hadn't really felt like playing at all.

'When's mama coming back home?'

I held her hand tight but couldn't look at her as I had to pay attention to the road. Which was for the best.

'Soon,' I lied. 'Very soon.'

Secretly, I had hoped her visit might make a difference. Her voice, her touch, her smell. But Zanele didn't respond. Shanla kept trying. 'Mama, mama', she whispered, as if she knew there was no point speaking loudly.

Seeing Shanla beside the bed, with her mother's hand folded in hers, made me sad. But I couldn't give in to sadness. That wouldn't help Shanla or me. I hated it when these feelings welled up in me. They didn't suit me. I had suffered from them before when I was still a child, like Shanla. Then I, too, would call out for my mother, scared to lose her. But what would become of Shanla?

Mbufu, I knew, would go his own way. But Shanla?

No one would accept her remaining with me, in a white house. I'd like it, but her uncles and aunts wouldn't, nor would her grandmother and her father. Her father? One way or another, black fathers always came to know these things and, at least temporarily, would assume a paternal role. I mustn't set myself against it — again I saw Zanele's deep eyes in the drying shop. Don't mix, she'd explained to me; it was better that way, more sensible. She was probably right. I shouldn't be naïve.

They'd find Shanla a place with relatives — far away. She would be absorbed into another family, and her mother's image would slowly fade. I hoped she would try and hang on to it, to remember how it had been: Zanele preparing our food, walking barefoot along the path. I knew what would happen to Shanla. But not to me.

It dragged on a week longer than we expected. No, there was no hope. If it had been one of my patients, that's what I would have had to say to the family. Now I said it to myself. I shouldn't harbour any illusions; it was only a question of time. I returned home every day. Shanla still slept in their room. I'd asked her if she wanted to sleep inside, but that seemed strange to her. She would sleep in Zanele's room as usual — alone now, but soon with Zanele again. I nodded; I didn't want to disillusion her. Anyway, Mbufu often slept in the room, and she liked that. I prepared dinner for Shanla and had to cook it myself. I didn't even know how. All the years of sitting, watching on the bench, and now I didn't even know how to do things the way Shanla liked them. The plate of *milliemeal* was the only easy thing. Shanla came to get her plate and tapped my back. 'Joni?'

I turned around.

'Your bracelet, I've got it.'

The red stones glistened in the palm of her hand.

She smiled. 'Mama should wear.'

I bent over to get a better look at the bracelet. She held it in her hand as if it were a living thing that might fly away.

She didn't dare do it herself — her mother had told her that she mustn't ever touch it. Bad enough to have retrieved it from under the bed, but actually putting it on Zanele was going too far. I held the red bracelet and first let the tips of Zanele's index and middle fingers glide over the little balls.

She didn't react. I swallowed, and carefully placed it on her limp wrist. I felt her warmth. I was closer than usual, and held her wrist tightly for a bit longer.

'You're wearing it,' I whispered. I swallowed again.

She was wearing it for the first time but she couldn't see it. A shiver shot up my spine.

I'd asked about it so often. 'Save,' she'd say. In God's name, what for?

I wanted to tell her how it suited her. I wanted to tell her again that I'd chosen it for her because of the beautiful red colour. I'd told her what red was supposed to mean. It's so nice to finally see it on you, I thought, as I carefully closed the catch.

'Don't ever take it off,' I whispered in her left ear.

My fingers still lay on her hand, against the red stones. I placed my other hand underneath, so that her wrist could rest between.

'Zanele?'

Everything made me sad. And the fact that I couldn't tell her that, saddest of all. My head sank onto the white sheets.

Stay with me—please.

It was only after I'd shut my eyes that I heard a child crying. I immediately sat upright. I had made a child cry. Damn.

As I'd expected, they came to get Shanla—six people I'd never seen before in a minibus. Shanla knew them, which was reassuring. Mbufu would get a lift with them to a friend's place in a township. He told me that he had spoken to Gibsan, and he'd said he could go on working at my house if I wanted him to. I never wanted to see him again.

I'd told Albert that he'd have to start looking for a replacement for me. But now that Shanla was ready, bags packed, I thanked God I was still on shift.

Zanele's family members didn't appear especially miserable or sad; it was as if all this had happened before. They embarked on hearty discussions with Mbufu about the best route to the township. Another youth, a cousin I assumed, shooed a butterfly away as if it was a wasp. It was only then that I realised what month it was.

With a stabbing sensation in my stomach, I gave Shanla two kisses, and she hugged me. She pressed me tightly against herself. 'Poppet,' I whispered.

I asked the man standing near us, who had introduced himself as an uncle, if he could give me a postal address. He shook his head. In Zulu, he told me that they couldn't receive any mail. Did he have a telephone, I asked. He yelled to his wife, and they started bickering. I couldn't follow what they were saying. Mbufu stepped in, and I got a number. Whose number it was wasn't clear, but Mbufu said I should write it down. 'I'll remember it. Just give it to me.'

Could I maybe give Shanla some money, asked the man who'd introduced himself as her uncle, and still stood nearby. I'd prepared for this. I handed over an envelope in which there was only a small sum. Before they'd come, we'd hidden money in Shanla's bag. Zanele had at least taught me never to give money to a man. Shanla would guard it closely and never hand it over. She had my numbers and details with it, and if I moved I told her I'd try and let her know. When Mbufu called from the path that they were ready to leave, I

179

quickly pressed a kiss on her forehead.

Slowly, Shanla got into the minibus. Mbufu didn't kiss me. I didn't know whether it was because he didn't dare with the guys there, or that he just didn't feel like it. I collapsed into my car—I wanted to be the first to drive away.

My lower lip was trembling. To make sure they didn't see it, I waved as hard as possible with my right hand close to my face.

The morning sun had trouble climbing. Usually it took only minutes, but today it took forever.

I wanted to give Albert my notice and let him know that, temporarily, he couldn't count on me.

I stepped into the shower—I could feel a headache coming on. I remembered the supply of painkillers that I'd carefully collected over the years. I'd take a couple as I was getting dried. I was frustratingly slow washing myself; even my arm didn't seem to work any more. But I couldn't give in—patients would be coming in all day, the wounded on a conveyor belt. I had to pull myself together in order to be useful, just as I'd learnt at home. Dizzy, I walked out of the shower. I wrapped a towel around my body and knotted it under my armpit. I looked in the mirror. I hadn't seen that expression in a long time.

I bent over. The tablets were in the bathroom cabinet. Straightening up, I started to stagger. I took a deep breath and quickly threw them down with tap water.

There was a comb next to the wash basin, but I didn't want to look in the mirror again. I quickly combed my hair into place without checking the result. It didn't matter anyway. I sank onto the bed. Dress—I had to dress myself.

I hadn't opened the curtains. But I hadn't properly shut them, either. In the meantime, the sun had reached its highest point. A white stripe shone in on my right leg. I remembered Zanele, and how once the sun had turned her white—how beautiful I'd thought it was. The tablets weren't helping. Nauseated, I tried to chase away my memories.

Downstairs, I walked into the kitchen. It stank. Something had been there for too long. I stood waiting for the water to boil, with my heavy forehead leaning against the kitchen cupboard.

The knob on the kettle had popped up without my hearing it. I lifted the kettle, and poured water over the coffee grains and stirred for a long time. With a worsening headache, I went into the living room. I stood by the big garden window, the warm mug in my hands. The grass was too long and the plants unkempt. They were thirsty. Clearly thirsty. I should get the bucket that Zanele used as a watering can, I thought, as I looked at the silence of the garden. I took a sip of hot coffee. The silence of the house.

Make myself useful. Useful.

Leaving the half-empty mug behind, I walked towards the naked man. My car keys were in the ugly dish on his head. I'd need money, too. Or my bag—maybe that was easier. It was lying waiting for me under the stairs. Had I put it there? Bending over, I almost collapsed, and I was shocked by how weak I was. I saw the skinny legs of a child. A small child.

Once behind the steering wheel, though, the same leg displayed an unexpected strength. I drove far too fast through the turn, after which I couldn't hold the accelerator back and shot out onto the dirt road. On the main road, I set course for the hospital. I parked close to the entrance, and gave two rand to the usual young beggar limping up to me.

I walked into the building.

A huge resistance welled up in me. Why must I go on working? Who for? I'd never once asked myself that. Who for, in God's name? I felt the beads of sweat popping up under my fringe. I felt clammy. Was it hotter than normal?

My ears started ringing. I had to leave the hospital—but I was on shift. As I walked to my department, I felt myself slowing down. My thighs got heavier; they were in danger of not making it.

With difficulty, I managed to turn 180 degrees. Yes, away again. Whenever I couldn't cope. Wouter. Papa, Mama. Why must you always be seen to be coping? I'd tell my own children that that's what life is about—coping. I was soaked to the skin. It was an idea—the idea that everyone must be able to cope. At the sight of the main entrance I could already breathe easier.

The begging Afrikaan was talking; no one noticed me. My heavy legs walked back to the car. They wanted to give way, collapse. I hated the body that was letting me down. The only strength I still had was in my right hand, which tightly clenched the bunch of keys. The pointy end of a key stuck into my skin. I felt nothing. Only longing.

Hold me for a moment. If you hold me just for a moment, I can let myself go. I opened the door and stepped in.

My head sank back against the head support. He asked what I was still so afraid of.

'Nothing, nothing.'

He stroked my cheek.

I felt his questioning eyes.

That Zanele is gone, I told him. He has taken her from me. All the years I thought that he would come for me, but he had something worse in store—he took Zanele. 'And he glided peacefully on, above the land, between the stars and sometimes on the ground, here, between the people and the animals.'

Carefully, he brushed my hair from my face. I wasn't sure, but I felt, noticed, that he had touched my face. That means that he is here. He should hold me, protect me. My body shivered while I didn't dare move.

There was a tapping on my window. Almost friendly, as if we knew each other, the young beggar smiled broadly. I sat behind the wheel, sweating, the car keys still in my hand. I gestured with my hand that he would get no more from me. He didn't go away. Despite the trembling in my legs, it looked like I'd have to drive away.

I walked into the hallway without wiping away the drops of urine. I hadn't washed my hands, either. I opened the kitchen door, and the stench of rotting rubbish engulfed me. My eyes fell on the rubbish bin. How often had my feet …? It must be full of rats now.

There was an enormous pressure above my eyes; my forehead pounded under my fringe. Damn, I heard something. Hadn't I shut the front door properly? No, I heard something on the path. Who could be on our path now? Footsteps. I hurried to the external kitchen door and unlocked it with difficulty. I couldn't see anything unusual.

I could barely feel my legs, and had to sit for a moment there on the path. My knees gave way, my face—little more than cheekbones—in my hands.

'You here?'

I started.

I squinted and held my right hand up against the sun. Because he was standing right in the bright light, I couldn't bring him into focus.

How come I looked so awful? I didn't know what I looked like. There was silence again, and I sensed his discomfort.

Should he take me inside? My head shook. I was fine—I didn't need to be taken anywhere.

I could see his face under his hat—unshaven as usual. He looked surprised. I wanted to ask if he would sit for a while, here, beside me—at last, sitting together on the path in daylight. He was so tall, so big. He stood and I sat, but I couldn't get up. I didn't have the strength. What brought him here?

Did I want something to eat or drink, he asked.

I smiled, dry lips pressed together. I lived here; if I wanted something, I'd get it. This body didn't need anything.

He sat beside me. Brightly, he pulled something from his pants pocket, but I couldn't see what it was. It was only as he opened the palm of his hand and held it in front of me that I understood why he was here. Shanla had apparently forgotten to take it with her after she had brought it back from the hospital. The red stones glistened in the sun.

'Ten rand, or maybe twenty, I will get.'

My body summoned all its strength to grab it from his palm. He stopped me and gripped me tightly, but it barely hurt. Quickly, he shoved the bracelet back in his pocket. But he didn't let me go. Calmly, he watched me while his right hand pushed aside my hair.

My head slid to his shoulder. He said he had to get going, and stood up.

So that's what the night-people looked like during the day.

Eyes closed, I let my head fall back against the wall. I felt the warmth of the sun on my face. My body trembled. I heard him say goodbye.

I remained seated, waiting for the warmth to free me.

The steel gate fell shut, and I heard something jingling. His mother's keys.

It dawned on me that I'd never had the gate key.

I'd never used that gate, of course—but I should at least have the key. He'd taken it with him, and who knows who would come and visit me in the middle of the night. I got up, rushed to the gate, and called angrily after him. He walked on. Screaming into the wind, I shook the locked gate back and forth like a lunatic. My head pounded the steel, but I didn't feel it. I pounded harder, so the jolts could stream through my body.

Again, he had shown me that I was nothing—meant nothing.

I had to get up, not allow myself to be overcome.

I took a couple of steps and opened the kitchen door to the house. My body didn't want to go back inside; there was nothing for it there.

But there wasn't anything for it out here, either.

The path didn't connect anything any more. It was deathly silent—except for the noise from my stomach—and as empty as the cloudless sky. No dancing feet—the door knob slid from my hands—no rustling papers. Only emptiness. Here I'd stay. Trembling. My breathing quickened, at first in my throat, then through my whole head. I tried to check it, but couldn't, and my heart assumed the same rhythm. The trembling grew stronger. The emptiness around me frightened me. The power of nothingness was too much and threatened to overwhelm me. My head swam. Someone must help me. I staggered to the gate. I shouldn't have let her go. I could no longer breathe. Where are you? They would neglect her. Mama, where are you? My throat closed over.

Gulping for breath, I reached the closed gate. I should never have left him. We should have dared, together. He didn't dare. I shook the gate back and forth, trying, with my fists around the steel, to still hang on to something. I called into the wind, but no one heard me.

I was jeered at—loudly jeered at. Immediately, I let go of the gate. My hands shook, and my heart no longer knew any moderation. I worried that it would beat itself to death, here, on the path. Faster and faster. I lay flat on my stomach so that I could press my face against the pavers. He mustn't see how afraid I was. Who I was—afraid of my own fear. The touch of the path, on which I'd sat so freely, hurt. No one must see that. My face scraped across the rough surface, grazing my skin.

Half rising, I lifted my head. My right hand felt my face. My heartbeat frightened me; I wasn't able to cope with this. So as not to fall, I had to move myself against the external wall. Now I was sitting, his grip on me strengthened, and his hands tried to squeeze my throat. I was in danger of choking.

The need to breathe became urgent. The flow of blood to my head was scarcely enough. My body began to twitch.

This was my punishment. I hadn't protected myself. Someone nodded. I don't know who, but someone nodded. My body cowered beneath my clothes, soaked from head to toe, and cold droplets slid from my forehead and down my cheeks. My fringe was plastered against my wet forehead. Trembling, I brushed it aside. The laughter was deafening, and a powerful voice began speaking.

That voice—I knew it now. 'Take a good look', said the God of Africa. 'You can't hide any more.'

His clamour jolted through me and stuck in my heart. Never before had he been so close. My soaked head sank, my knees pressed against my ears, but nothing shut out his annihilating laughter. Nothing.